MAGICK THIEF

THE ORDER OF FATE
BOOK 1

TAVITA LANE

For all the girls with a little magick in their blood.

1

Cassie

She dragged the door open. It was hard enough to get past the wards in the first place. Cassie didn't want to give herself away over a creaky door.

The room was dark and the vibration of magick was stronger than she'd felt in a long time. It was not just piquing her interest, but intoxicating.

She moved past the dark wood tables set to the side of the room and the books stacked on top of them. One fell from the top of the massive pile and opened. She slide her gaze to it and squinted. Something was weird about that book. It seemed to hold all the magick she was feeling, even though it wasn't what she was here for.

She ignored it and moved to the far side of the room. She realized the room was paneled and made a face.

Why would you do that?

She rested her hand on the wall and closed her eyes. The sound of the magick fought with her senses. It had a cadence most people wouldn't expect, almost like a heart-beat of its own.

With her own magick, she pushed at it until she heard a click on the other side. The wall split open and Cassie pushed her hand through. She grabbed the small metal pen. Her hand felt like it was on fire. She almost dropped it, but somehow held on even though her hand felt like she'd stuck it on a burner and thought, yeah, I'll wait and see what this does.

She pulled her hand back through the wall and tossed the pen into her bag. Her gaze slid to the book that had garnered so much interest a few minutes prior. Cassie bit her lip. What harm would it do to take this one other thing as well?

She took a step and surveyed the book. It was sitting on its spine, open to a page she didn't understand, but the power. That was what was amazing about it. There had to be something more to it.

She grabbed it and her breath stopped. It was full of so much magick. It was almost overwhelming. She almost didn't notice the barrel of the shotgun on her back. Almost.

"Put it down," a sophisticated man said from behind her. Even his voice sounded like it was rich.

She put the book on a nearby table and put her hands up. She closed her eyes for a moment, letting her magick survey the situation. He was in close proximity, with the gun cocked, but it was clear that he hadn't fired one in a long time. At least, that was what she figured.

She let her blue eyes flutter open and spun on him. Before he could even think of pulling the trigger, she had the gun knocked out of his hands.

"Sorry about this," she said as she raised her hand and a blue line encased him on the floor. It wrapped around him until it met and then rose, encasing him in a blue bubble of sorts.

"It won't last too long," Cassie turned and grabbed the book, even with protests from Mr sophisticated in the bubble.

"You don't understand what that book is, do you?" He said, watching her.

She turned and took him in for the first time. He was older, probably in his fifties, with short graying hair. He was wearing a suit even at this time of night. She figured he hadn't gone to bed yet.

"And you do?"

"I do. I've been studying magick for a long time."

"Great, but it doesn't look like you have any."

Cassie raised her hand, and fire sat in her palm. "I think I'll be fine."

"You have no idea."

His words sent a shiver up her spine, but she ignored it. Cassie closed her hand, and the fire went out before she turned and walked through the door and out of the house.

Cassie slipped the book into the bag with the pen and slung it over her shoulder. The magick made her back tingle, but she had the goods. Now all she needed was a buyer.

Cassie smiled. She was aware of the pen. The person who requested it had been quite forthcoming about its purpose. Your future could be written by that damn thing. It couldn't affect others, but it could give you anything you wanted and make every dream come true. That was a power Cassie did not know why anyone would want. Sure, it sounds fine, but all magick has a cost of some kind. The Order had taught her that.

She shook her head at the thought. Cassie had fought to

get out of that mess. The thing that had destroyed her family, she didn't want anything to do with it.

She was so far in thought; she didn't feel the magick ripple around her until it was too late. Cassie was taking a hit and eating the concrete. She spun quickly and kicked at the person who had knocked her down.

They flew back and their dark hood fell onto their back. She met Cassie's eyes and hissed at her. Cassie shook her head. Fucking Vampires.

"You realize I'm not in the Order anymore, right?" She pulled herself to her feet and raised her hands in frustration at the Vamp Woman.

"Once you're in, you don't leave. You'll always be my enemy." She glanced at the bag and then back to her. "Besides, you have something we want."

We? She felt the change in the air before she saw him. He was old. Probably one of the older vampires she's seen. Cassie shook her head. Why are they always vampires? Cassie had dealt with a lot of different types of demons, but these were the oldest ones. Some say beginning evil.

"I don't want to hurt you, Cassie, but I will," the man said as he got closer. She couldn't see him clearly until he was almost in front of her. Then she saw him. His dark eyes locked on her and his old west style clothing made her knit her brow in confusion. Did he just like looking like he was from the old west?

"Look, I don't want you to hurt me either, but you're not getting that book." She tightened her grip on the bag and slid it over her shoulder.

"You don't know what it is, do you?" He said, cocking his head to one side.

"Don't care, but if you want it, I want it more." She reached inside of herself and pulled at the magick in her.

She felt it twist around her until it rested in her palm. She smiled as she twitched her hand and fire formed between her and the Vampire.

Cassie knew she couldn't take on two vampires on her own, much less one that was as old as this guy. She bolted down the road as fast as she could and turned the corner, but he was faster and blocked her way. She ran into him as he grabbed her wrist and threw her against the wall of an alley she'd gone down without thinking.

"Magick is fine if you know how to use it," he said, getting closer to her.

"Who said I didn't? Maybe I just don't want to use it on you," Cassie snapped.

"Then you're stupid," he said. "Give me the book. This is your last chance."

Cassie pulled herself to her feet and ignored the nagging pain in her left leg. She couldn't run now. "No."

He shook his head. "What a waste." He came at her, grabbing her arm and pulling the bag away from her. Once he had it in his hands, he gave her a hard shove back into the wall and pulled the bag open. His gaze went back to Cassie. "Where is it?"

"I put it in there, I swear," she said before closing her eyes. She felt her heartbeat quicken and the magick rise inside her. She let it fill her until it was begging to escape, to find a way out. She opened her eyes and let it go. The charge in the air made her ears ring, but the power was intoxicating. The Vamp realized what was happening right before the magick tore through his skin. It pushed him to the ground as the ripple hit the woman Vamp with him. She disintegrated in front of Cassie's eyes.

Cassie grabbed the bag and hobbled away as fast as she could around a corner before leaning on the wall and casting a glamor so no one could see her. She waited, holding her breath and trying to ignore the pain tearing through her.

The Vampire turned the corner and stopped. A smile crossed his lips. "Magick can't hurt me. I know you're still here."

Cassie felt her breath catch as she tried to stay quiet. Then she felt something else and knew her little game was over.

* * *

She watched as this vampire with so much more power than she'd ever seen before looked her dead in the eye. A smile crept to his lips, and he brought his hand up to grab the bag over her shoulder.

She couldn't back up, so she braced for this vampire to kill her, or worse. Instead, he froze and turned around slowly. She followed his gaze to someone she really didn't want to see.

"That's enough, Wes," he said.

The Vampire turned and eyed the man standing behind him. He looked the same as he had the last time she'd seen him. Cody wore dark jeans and a dark blue long-sleeved shirt. His glasses sat on his nose and his dark hair was short, just the same as always. His light eyes fixed on Cassie before sliding to the Vampire.

"Cody, you just won't give up, will you?" He stood in front of Cassie, blocking her against the wall. "This one is mine."

"No, she's not. She's a part of the Order. You know that."

"Do I?" He said with a smile.

"Do you really want a war with us?" Cody stepped

forward, and a woman came into view behind him. Cassie groaned as she realized who it was.

Wes cocked his head and slid his gaze to the woman and back to Cody. "You'd do better to keep your people out of my side of town. You never know what will happen over here. It's easy to get lost." He smiled and then was gone before Cassie could blink.

Cody crossed his arms and took a step towards her. "What did he want?"

She shrugged. "I don't know." Cassie pulled the bag closer to her. She didn't know if he could see through her glamor, but she was going to keep this haul as close as possible.

"When did you get back?" the woman asked.

"Sorry, sis. I just didn't want to make it a thing," Cassie said, stepping out of her hiding place.

"A thing?" She shook her head. Her light brown hair shaking down her back.

"Look Lark, you were always the better sister. We both know that," Cassie said.

She grabbed Cassie's arm and stopped her from her getaway. "That's not true."

"Sure it is. Mom always said you had the magick and you could follow orders like you're supposed to. I'm just not built like that." Cassie pulled her arm away and turned, but Cody was standing in front of her.

Oh, come on!

"Come back to headquarters with us. Let me make sure you're okay and then you can do whatever it is you want to." His light eyes peeled her defenses away, and she nodded her head reluctantly.

She was shaken up. She'd never met a demon she couldn't kill.

"Who the hell was that vampire?"

Cody flinched at the question, but keep walking.

"He was someone you don't want to be caught in a dark alley with," Lark answered for him. "If you'd stayed at the Order, you'd know all about him."

She rolled her eyes, but kept walking. Her sister was always the one that knew everything. She was five years older and made sure everyone knew. When Cassie joined the order, she was only fifteen. Her sister and mom had already been protecting humanity for several years. Cassie trained for three years before she got to go on her first mission, but everything went wrong and they lost the one person they both had felt like they could trust.

Their mother.

Cassie quit the next day, but Lark seemed to think it was her new mission to protect anyone she could, no matter the cost.

They turned the corner and the Order's headquarters came into view. It was a simple building in the middle of a dark and sometimes dangerous city. It always reminded Cassie of a church, but the symbols were nothing like that. No crosses or other Christen items. Our history was buried deep in Apache tradition. All our legends and protections came from there. The original elders didn't see the race. They only saw potential.

The old brick was still looking worse for wear as each day progressed, but she still respected the work. It just wasn't for her.

They walked into the building and everything expanded. The ceiling looked taller and the building suddenly had way more room.

"You gotta love Magick," Cassie said as she took in the tall ceiling. The light leaked through, even though it was night. The walls were exposed brick, with bookshelves lining the far wall of the room. A young man with blond hair walked past and looked at Cassie. He looked almost confused that she was with Cody.

Cody ran the entire Order of Fate now, or The Order for short.. There were a lot of rumors as to what happened, but he never really spoke about it. Lark was second in command and I was certain she knew everything he was willing to tell, but wasn't going to say anything to me.

"My office, please," Cody said, waving us towards the old wood door. Lark stepped in first and Cassie followed. Cody closed the door behind them and they all sat at the desk.

"Now that we're someplace where eyes and ears are not, I can talk to you." He walked to the other side of the desk and watched Cassie. "What did you take?"

"Just a pen," Cassie said. She wasn't going to give up the book. It was something she wanted to figure out on her own.

He eyed her, and she didn't break her stance. The last thing Cassie wanted was for Cody to know what she was doing. She figured changing the subject was a better idea.

"Who was that vampire? You didn't answer me earlier," Cassie asked.

Cody stopped and dropped his gaze to his desk. He took a long time to say anything. "He's someone I knew a long time ago."

"A long time ago?" Cassie asked.

"Yes. That's the only reason he was any leeway at all." Cody sat and shook his head. "The last thing you want is any problems with Wesley."

"He's different from other vampires," she said.

"Yes, he is." Cody met her gaze, and it made Cassie shiver. "Never forget that."

"Cassie, you should probably stay here tonight. They

might be looking for you," Lark said. "I don't want anything to happen to you."

"You do realize I've been taking care of myself on my own for two years." Cassie glared at Lark.

"Not with a vampire. you can't defend yourself against looking for you," she snapped.

"Fine. I'll stay till dawn, but then I'm out of here," Cassie said, standing and looking at Cody. "Is my room still empty?"

"No, but mom's room is," Lark said. "You can stay there tonight."

"Perfect," Cassie sighed. That's just where she wanted to stay, in the place of her dead mother's room.

She opened the door and walked away.

2

Cody

He sat at his desk and sighed. It had been so long since he'd seen Wesley. They'd made the truce work, but he feared maybe it was something he should have stayed away from. What good could come from a truce that was formed so long ago?

* * *

Arizona 1898

They sat around the fire, watching it pop in the darkness. Cody loved the silence that came with the night in the desert. It was the only home he'd known, and Maggie was the only person he felt connected to since leaving the Order of Fate.

She glanced at him; her waving red hair falling into her face slightly. He smiled at her. Maggie wasn't a witch like him, but she was strong and able to defend herself from any demon they'd come up against before. This time it was different, though. They had to destroy the evil that had taken his friend Wesley and his mentee, Ami.

Even though it had been a long time since he'd worked with Wesley, he still felt like he owed him.

Cody threw a stick at the fire and sighed. "I don't think I can hunt, my friend."

"Then don't. There are others in the Order that can do it. Why does it have to be you?"

Cody met Maggie's gaze. "I was there when it happened. I could have stopped it."

"How?" Maggie said. "It happened so fast and Wesley made a choice." She got up and walked to him. She plopped down on the dirt beside him and pulled him to her. "There was nothing you could have done differently. It just happened."

"This kind of thing doesn't just happen," Cody said. He leaned into her and pulled her closer. She smiled. "I'm glad I met you through this, though."

She leaned in and kissed him. He smiled.

"Let's just take this day by day," she whispered. "Don't think about the future. At least not right now."

3

Cassie

Cassie stood at the white wood door, just staring at it. She hadn't been here since her mother died.

She slowly opened the door and took in the room.

She glanced at the bed, still sitting in the center of the room. Its old white wood looked somehow more worn than it did just two years ago. The stone walls still had the photos of her and her sister hung on them. The frames still held that dark brown color.

Cassie held her breath before she closed the door and stepped back into the hallway.

I can't do this.

Cassie wondered the hallways for a while, just thinking about why she was even still here. She could just leave, no one would miss her. Except maybe Lark, but that was a bridge she didn't know if she could ever mend.

She didn't notice the girl at the end of the hallway until she smacked into her.

"Sorry," Cassie said before looking at her. The girl was young, maybe fifteen, with dark eyes and long black hair. She was shorter, but she stood tall as Cassie took her in.

"I haven't seen you here before," she said, raising an eyebrow.

"I'm just visiting."

"I'm Sanora," she said. Sanora leaned against the wall behind her and stared at Cassie. "You don't look anything like your sister."

Cassie snapped her gaze up. "How do you know about my sister?"

She shrugged. "You hear things around here."

"I'm not staying." Cassie folded her arms across her chest.

"Why?" Sanora watched her as she spoke.

"I don't have to tell you my life story."

"No, but you have one or you wouldn't be here. Where all the weird people are."

"Are you a witch?" Cassie was interested now.

"No. Are you?"

Cassie thought about how to answer. A lot of the people here were witches, but there was a stray human or other creature. Mostly, Werewolves.

"I'm a witch." Cassie glanced past her and almost groaned at the sight of a light-haired guy she'd known from years ago. He hadn't seen her yet, so she still had a chance to escape if she could just get past Sanora.

"Well, I gotta go." Cassie hurried backwards down the hall she'd came down, hoping she could make the turn before he saw her.

"Cassie?" The voice made her cringe. This was the last thing she was expecting when she agreed to stay here after all this time.

She took a breath and spun around. "Brandon, how have you been?"

The blonde smiled and settled his gorgeous green eyes on her. She forced a smile. The last time she'd seen him, he was running from a water demon.

"I'm doing well. Are you back?"

"No, I'm not back," Cassie snapped. She took in the boy she'd known and trained with. He had for sure muscled out in the last two years and, if it was possible, his eyes had gotten greener. His light hair was still a bit messy, but it made him look even better.

"I was hoping you would be back for good. This place isn't the same without you."

"How so?" Cassie was interested now. She liked knowing what was going on at the Order, even if she didn't want to be a part of it.

"Cody has been acting really strange. He's recruiting at a rate I've never seen, but the difference is he's looking for witches specifically."

"It makes sense. Witches have more to offer when hunting demons." She shrugged.

"Maybe, but it's also thinning out the Witch community. You know how it is. Not many families left to work with."

"Maybe." Cassie knew what he'd meant. When the Order started, there were mostly humans that fought. Slowly Witches have seemed to fill up the recruits more and more, especially since Cody had started running it.

"I gotta go," Cassie said without stopping to give Brandon a chance to sway her. She wasn't interested in reliving her past, even if it was interested in her.

Cassie wondered around until the place was for the most part empty. There were a few stray people walking the halls that would stare at her and whisper, but she ignored them. A part of her wondered how many people thought she was back.

She stopped at the big training area. It was empty, so she figured she would get a little privacy there to take a look at her haul.

Cassie still had the book that had called to her in her bag. She felt it every time she thought about magick or what it would be like to read it. She still had no idea what it was. She slid it out of her bag and said the enchantment that would allow it to be seen again. The old tattered book shimmered to reality in her hands.

Cassie ran her hand over it and the light hum of magick made her hand vibrate. She slid her fingers over the cover and pulled it open.

The words were in a language she didn't recognize, but it whispered in her head. She started seeing pictures of war and people dying all around her. She was standing in a field. Gun fire was in the background. She couldn't tell from where, but it was there. The smell of burning flesh filled her nose. She put her hand up to her face to try to filter it out, but couldn't. She gagged and coughed until her body was used to the rotting smell.

Cassie took a step and had to step over a body dead on the ground. She couldn't tell if it was a man or woman, as the entire face was ripped clean from the body. When she looked up, she saw a large wolf looking at her. She stood still, unsure of where she was or why it was watching her. She didn't even understand why it was here in the first place. This was not a place for wolves.

It showed its teeth and glared. She didn't take her eyes off of it.

"It's okay. I'm not sure where I am." Cassie held her hands up to show she wasn't a threat.

It didn't move, but she felt cold all of the sudden and felt her body fall to the ground.

Her eyes fluttered open, and the pounding in her head caught her attention.

What the hell was that?

Her eyes slid to Cody standing in the doorway. His eyes went from her to the book in her hands, and he shook his head.

"I knew you still had it," he said before walking towards her.

She dropped it onto the floor and shook her head. "I don't want anything to do with it."

"Interesting, it connected to you. Not everyone gets to read it." Cody scooped it up and put it on the seat beside them.

"I didn't read it." Cassie rubbed her throbbing head.

"No?"

"No, it was more like I was someplace else." Cassie stared at it and shook her

Head. "It was weird. I was standing in this field with dead bodies and a wolf staring dead at me."

"How is that possible?" Cody looked as confused as Cassie felt. He ran his hand through his hair and sighed.

"What aren't you telling me?"

"There are things that no one knows. Not Lark, not anyone at the Order. No one." Cody finally met her gaze.

"Okay?" She wrinkled her forehead in confusion.

"That book is safer here and you with it. Now that you've opened it, you're connected."

"So, I just won't look at it again," Cassie joked.

"It doesn't work that way. You really should have left it alone."

Cassie had no clue what Cody was talking about, but the

look on his face said he was worried and he was never worried.

"I'll have them clean out your mother's room. Lark should have never suggested you stay there when it hasn't been touched in years."

"It's okay. I would like to clean it. There might be something still there for my mothers." Cassie felt the dread of going back there all through her body, but she couldn't hide from it.

"Lark hasn't been in there. Maybe you could do it together. Maybe it would be a little easier."

"Have you met my sister?" Cassie gave him a look. "Nothing is ever easy

with her."

Cody stood. "Get some rest. We don't know how this book is going to affect you long term," he said with a tone of caring. His light brown hair fell into his face and made him look more human than he had in a long time.

Cassie sighed. She knew he was right, and that meant she was back for more than she wanted to be.

Great.

She walked back down the hallway towards her mother's old room. No, she didn't want to stay there, and she wasn't going to. Cassie headed past it and towards her sister's room. Her room was just down the hall and if she knew her, which she did, she would stay in that room as long as she could. Cassie would just sleep on her floor and listen to her lecture about the book later. She could at least hope Cody hadn't told her what she'd been doing with it. Not yet.

Cassie stopped at the door marked 32 and knocked. She listened for footsteps, but didn't hear them right away. Great, she'd woke her up. The door knob turned and a usually well put together Lark was a mess with her hair pulled into a bun on her head. Pieces of her light brown hair were sticking out in all directions, and she barely had her eyes open.

"What are you doing here?"

"I can't stay in mom's room," Cassie said without missing a beat. "Can I just sleep on your floor?"

Lark opened her eyes more and sighed. She didn't say anything but moved to the side so Cassie could walk in. "You can stay on the couch. "

Cassie edged her way into the room and sat on the couch. She wanted to tell her sister everything, to be close again, but their sisterly bond had been broken when their mom died.

"Thanks." Cassie rubbed her eyes and hoped this time, when she laid down, sleep would come. The last place she wanted to be was back with that wolf. There was something weird about the whole thing. Cassie laid down and the lights in the room went off.

"We're going to have to talk about what's next in the morning." Lark laid in her bed and pulled the covers over her. She sat up just long enough for Cassie to see her watching her.

"I know," Cassie said. She turned over and stared at the ceiling for only a few.

moments before sleep took her.

Cassie heard loud talking and opened her eyes. She was still laying on Lark's couch but the door was open and Lark was fighting with someone. Cassie strained to listen.

"I'm not going back to that room. There are too many memories tied to it."

"Look, I'm just the messenger. Cody wants it cleared so Cassie has a place to stay," a male voice said.

"I just... I can't."

"Then you'll have to take it up with him." A pause. "What about Cassie?"

"What about her? You know how she is. One minute she wants to be here,

next she wants to use magick for herself."

"You should give her a break. You weren't the only one that lost a mother that day," the male voice said as she heard footsteps and the door closing. Cassie closed her eyes and waited a few seconds before fake waking up.

She slowly sat up and stretched. Lark turned to her and threw some clothes in her face.

"You should change. If you're going to be here, you have to do your job." Her tone was filled with snark and something else Cassie couldn't quite pinpoint. Annoyance? Jealousy?

Cassie looked at the clothes and rolled her eyes. "I can just go to my place and get some things."

"You'll have to get approval from Cody for that." Lark pulled her long, curly hair into a ponytail and turned away. "I have to go for a briefing with Cody and then figure out what to do about this vampire thing."

Oh crap, now she would know everything and hate me even more.

"You should ask Brandon to go with you after you get it cleared with Cody. He's one of our best now." Lark stopped and looked at Cassie. "I'm glad you're okay."

"Yeah, me too." Cassie dropped her gaze. "For what it's worth, I'm sorry about getting into trouble."

Lark shrugged. "I know." She turned to leave and stopped at the doorway.

"Are you planning on staying here?"

"I don't want to, but Cody wants me here." Cassie left out the part about the book and how she could now read the future with it, or something like that. "Well, Cody knows a lot more than we do, so I'd listen to him," Lark said before walking through the open door. Cassie watched for a moment before grabbing her bag and heading out the door. There was no way she was going to ask permission to go to her place.

Cassie walked through the streets without much effort. It was day time so the potential of vampires wasn't an issue. Of course, that didn't mean she was out of the woods. There were other demons that weren't so limited by the dark.

She turned the corner to her small apartment. It was on the third floor and the only way to get to it were the stairs that felt like they pointed straight up. Cassie didn't mind it, though. The rent was cheap, and she tried not to stay here much between her heist jobs and her social life. Both had been pretty dead lately.

She climbed to the top of the stairs and stopped at her door. It was weirdly quiet. There was no music from the guy downstairs and he was always playing something so loudly it shook the floor. Cassie hesitated with her keys in her hands before she finally slid it into the lock and turned it. The door opened inward, and she glanced at the living room before she stepped inside.

Everything seemed in order. Her clothing was thrown all over the floor and her bed was situated on the far left side under two skylights that filled half the room. Her couch stood in the center of the room across from a television she'd gotten as a trade from one of her first jobs.

Cassie walked to the pile of clothes and picked up a few things. She smelled them and made a face. She shrugged and shoved them into her bag. She stopped at a photo she had stuck in her mirror. Her mother's face smiled back at her and she bit her lip. She looked so young. Her light hair was blowing away from her face as she held Cassie in her arms. She was maybe a year old in the photo and Lark was standing behind them with her arms crossed. Cassie couldn't help but smile.

She snatched the picture off the mirror and slid it into her bag. Cassie has no idea if she was going to be coming back here anytime soon. She almost missed the water dripping in her doorway. It was the smell that got her attention. The sulfur curled around her and filled her nose. Cassie gagged at the initial whiff, but she pulled herself together. She turned around and watched as the water pooled in her doorway, a gray smoke rising from it.

She watched the water puddle build on itself until it formed a weird-looking man with dark green hair and reptile eyes. He was wearing a pair of cargo pants and a dark brown shirt.

"You really were that stupid," he hissed.

Cassie pulled the bag over her shoulder and shrugged. "I don't have it."

"You mean the book?" He shook his head. "Don't need that now."

"Then why are you here?" Cassie kept her eyes on him as he eyed the doorway. Demons couldn't enter a human home without an invitation. That little piece of lore worked for all demons.

"Sweetheart, you are the key to the future now."

"I don't know what you are talking about," Cassie said. She held her ground, but was a little uneasy. If he was there, how many more were out there?

"You do, or you're really that stupid."

"Yeah, yeah, I'm stupid. Is that the best insult you have?"

He leaned in the doorway and looked at his hands. "You connected with the book. Now it works through you."

"That weird book you all seem to want? Yeah, it's not a great trip."

"Cody didn't tell you what happened to you, did he?"

Cassie cocked her head slightly. Now she was interested.

The Demon smiled. "That's the problem with the Order. They only tell you what they want you to hear."

"So, then tell me," Cassie said.

"When you connected with the book, you became a part of it. You became something bigger than a witch."

He still wasn't telling her anything. She threw her hands up and let them hit her sides.

"No one wants to tell me anything. Why?" She shook her head. "Look, this conversation has been fun and all, but I've got places to be." She raised her hand, and the Demon watched with a smile on his face.

"Relax, I'm not here to hurt you."

"Then why?"

"I'm for free information and all that." He shrugged before turning away from her. "Don't trust anyone, Cassie. It will get you killed."

"Because I'm going to take advice from you." Cassie watched as he turned to water and disappeared. This day was getting better and better.

4

Ami

Ami watched the doorway for them. She'd waited a long time to find the book and if Wesley didn't have it, she would have to find it herself. She pulled the hair tie from her hair and let it fall on her back. The time she'd spent as a vampire had made her hair thicker and more beautiful than it was when she was on the other side.

Wesley pushed the door open and met her gaze. He looked troubled, and Ami knew instantly he'd failed.

"It got away," she said before taking a seat on her four-poster bed. The only remnant of her past and the life she'd once had.

"A witch has it and Cody," he trailed off.

"Cody." She snapped her head to take him in. "Why didn't you kill him?"

"You know the rules," Wesley said. He took a seat beside her and gently stroked her cheek. "He is nothing but a thorn. The book is all that matters."

"Then why don't we have it?" She pushed his hand away. "I'm tired. This burden is too much."

"Then you should give it to me." Wesley didn't move.

"It doesn't work that way. You know that." She stood and walked to the chair on the other side of the room. She sat on it and stretched her legs. "I have to know what will happen."

"I'll find it and you'll know soon enough."

"I sent others to look during the day. It has to be found."

"We know where it is if Cody intercepted it," Wesley said. "We just can't get into the Order of Fate."

"Don't worry about that. I have a friend on the inside."

Wesley smiled. "You always do."

"When Price gave this to me," she faced Wesley and shook her head. "I didn't realize what it was going to be like. This immortality thing isn't a blessing and knowing you're this... thing. It's too much. I want out."

"We'll find the right one and transfer it soon."

"We have to."

5

Cassie

She made her way back to the Order of Fate, but instead of just going back to Lark's room or her mom's old one, she went straight for Cody's office. He had a lot to explain to her. She threw open his door and stood in the doorway. Lark and Cody both looked at her and she raised her eyebrows.

"We need to talk." Cassie crossed her arms and Lark's gaze slid from her to Cody.

"Please, shut the door." Cody said.

Cassie closed the door behind her and stood in front of it, arms crossed.

"What is it you need?" Cody said with annoyance in his voice.

She sighed and threw her hands up. "This book thing. You haven't told me everything, have you?"

Cody swallowed hard. He was for sure hiding something. "The book chose you."

"That much I got on my own. Why?"

"No one knows why it chooses who it does. It just does." Cody motioned for her to take a seat beside Lark. "It hasn't been seen in a really long time."

"I don't want it." Cassie looked at the seat and hesitated, but took it anyway. The soft fabric instantly made her feel better. She leaned back in it and for a moment forgot about all the crap going on.

"I don't know how it works. Not really, but I know Wes and Ami have been looking for it for a long time," Cody said.

"And you couldn't have said any of this before?" Cassie snapped.

"I didn't think it would come up like this," Cody said.

"That's the problem." Cassie shook her head. "What is it with the Vampires that you don't go after them like you do the others?"

Cody crossed his arms. "It's a long story."

"We have nothing but time," Cassie said.

He glanced from Lark to Cassie and shook his head. "A long time ago, I was expelled from the Order of Fate. I was living in the Desert of Arizona with my then girlfriend Maggie. One day, an old friend needed my help."

"What happened?" Lark said. She obviously didn't know about his past anymore than Cassie did.

"I helped him, but at a terrible cost." He sat and swallowed hard. "My friend was Wesley."

"So you were there when he turned into a vampire?" Cassie asked.

"We thought he could control it, but we were wrong."

"Then why do you give him the leeway you do now?" Cassie said. "You know what he is. If he's done this before, he's bound to come at us again."

"That's why I pick the people I do. They're stronger than just humans." Cody didn't look at Cassie.

"You think that witches can actually beat him?" Lark asked. "If you've been fighting him this long, then what makes you think it's different now?"

"The Order of Fate has never been this strong before. We have a chance."

"You mean now that I'm connected with the book?" Cassie jumped up and shook her head. "What is the big deal with it?"

"I told you. It shows the future. Whoever has it gets to know everything that will happen," Cody said.

"But I haven't seen anything except a weird wolf staring me down."

"So, you did see something." Cody seemed better with this change of subject. "Think. It's important to know."

"It... was more of a feeling and the smell of death. I don't know anything else."

"How can I when I don't know if I can trust you?"

"This is the only place where there are people you can trust," Lark chimed in.

"Why, because of our family history with the Order?" Cassie laughed. "Our mother died and I should have. Just because you feel like you need to be here doesn't mean I do." Cassie pulled open the door and walked from the room.

"You aren't safe out there on your own," Cody called behind her.

"Yeah, well, I'll take my chances." Cassie walked down the hallway past the others standing there watching the scenes play out and through the door.

"Cassie, they'll kill you for it," Cody said behind me. He seemed to not care that there were at least twenty pairs of eyes on him.

"And what about here?" Cassie shook her head. "How are we supposed to trust you when you leave half the story out?"

"I had to," Cody said.

"No you didn't. You chose to." Cassie opened the door and walked into the street. If she was going to have to deal with any kind of lying sneaky thing, it would be the demons that wanted that book. She took a deep breath and smelled the sulfur. And by the smell and looks of it, there were more than a few itching to say hi.

6

——————

Cody

He walked into his office and pulled out the last of the wooden stakes he'd hidden in the drawers. He didn't need them usually, but once Wes and Ami figured out Cassie was on her own, they would be coming for her. He may not be able to kill them, but he could slow them down. Maybe.

"What is she talking about?" Lark said, closing the door behind her.

"Something personal," he said, trying to make his way past her.

"I knew there was a past there, but I didn't know it was that involved." She locked eyes with him. "Did you know her?"

"I didn't know her well, but I went with what Wesley said. I trusted him." Cody shook his head.

"You formed a truce with them,: Lark said.

"I had no choice."

"You always have a choice," Lark said. "How long?"

"Longer than you've been alive." He pushed past her and through the door. "She's in more danger than you or I could know out there on her own."

"She isn't going to come back here now."

"No, not willingly." Cody didn't turn back to Lark.

"So, you're just going to force her back?"

"Sometimes we have to do things that are on the edge of what is right to keep everyone safe," Cody said.

"This is Cassie. This is my sister. I won't let you keep her as a prisoner."

"You don't have a choice." Cody nodded at the two older men by the door. They stepped forward, and each took a hold of Lark's arms. "I didn't want to do this, but we have to keep the world safe. That's what we were made for."

"You can't do this. The others won't allow it." Lark didn't bother fighting back. She knew the two older men had more magick than she did. They'd been at the Order for a long time. Hand picked by Cody himself.

"They don't have a choice."

* * *

ARIZONA 1898

CODY PULLED Maggie into a building at the edge of the small town they were in. The darkness of the night made everything seem that much more dangerous. Everything was quiet, but he knew something was wrong.

"They're here somewhere," he whispered. "We have to split up."

Maggie nodded. "I'll head to the other side of the street and sweep those houses." She smiled and took his head in her hands. "We'll find them and figure out what to do with Wesley after."

He nodded, and she ran out of the building. It was a small town, and Wesley and Ami couldn't be too far. Cody searched the building, but no one was there. It was odd considering the time of night it was. He walked out of the building slowly, but wasn't prepared for what he saw.

Standing in the center of the dirt street was Wesley, holding Maggie by her throat. He didn't move as Cody stepped towards him.

"Let her go," he said without stopping. "You don't want to do this."

"Are you sure, Cody." He sighed. "You act like you know me, but you don't know anything about me and what I want."

"I know you gave up everything for Ami," he said. "You let her turn you so you could stay together."

"What would you give up for Maggie?" Wesley said, giving her a yank. She let out a small whimper and Cody clenched his fists.

"What do you want?"

"I want you to leave me and Ami alone. The Order of Fate is gone. Let it go. Live your life with Maggie. Have babies and grow old. That's what you want, isn't it?" Wesley raised his eyebrow as he spoke.

"And if I say no?"

"Then you watch Maggie die and I won't kill you right away. I'll let you live with that, knowing you could have saved her. Until one day you beg for death," Wesley said with a smile.

"You were my friend once."

"That man is dead," Wesley said. "Make your choice."

Cody slid his gaze to Maggie, who was watching everything play out. She was innocent in all of this. While she was a part of the Order at one time, she had given it up to go with him and to help him. He had no right to ask any less of himself.

"I'll give you a truce, but you have to stay away from here and you can't kill any children ever."

Wesley smiled and let Maggie go. "Deal."

7

Cassie

Cassie kept herself at the ready. She knew she was now a huge target for anyone that wanted the book, even though she'd kept that information to herself. Stupid Demons. They seemed to know things before anyone else. She turned the corner and stopped short. Her eyes met something she'd never seen in real life.

The creature stepped out of the shadows and cocked its head at her. Cassie took a deep breath at the sight of the light-haired wolf. It studied her with its golden eyes and then looked past her at the dark smoke forming at the edge of the block.

Cassie turned and shook her head. She didn't want to be doing magick out in the open like this. Not when there were so many eyes on her. The wolf stepped up next to her before glancing her way and charging at the newly formed Demon. its red eyes and crooked smile were all Cassie saw before the Wolf was on top of it.

The Wolf bit through the Demon's extended arm and

threw it behind him, at Cassie's feet. She kicked it and watched the scene play out in front of her.

The Demon didn't have a chance to scream or thrash before the Wolf had its heart sitting on the pavement. Demons were once humans, so they still had what remained of their hearts. Even if they didn't use them anymore. It and Magick were one of their only weaknesses.

The Wolf turned back to Cassie before turning to walk away.

"Wait, you're the Wolf in my dreams. The one from the book," she said, taking a step towards it.

The wolf turned and eyed her with his golden eyes. She tried to read them, to see what was behind it and why they were connected. All she saw was pain.

It turned and ran away and Cassie was stuck standing there waiting for something to happen, but nothing did.

Cassie turned and walked into the old shop she was trying to get to. It was familiar, even though she hadn't been in it in years. The way the light shined through the windows and the faint hum of magick.

"Haven't seen you in a long while," a dark-haired, fair skinned woman popped her head up from behind the counter. There were odds and ends of magick all along it. Runes and crystals propped up at the back of it for display.

The store was what you would expect from a real witch. Not one of those new age weirdos that spouts peace and love. This was a place for those that knew what was really in the shadows and some of us who tried to stop it.

Cassie smiled as she closed the door behind her. "You saw me coming, huh?"

She laughed as Cassie spoke.

"Always. You know your mom is still looking out for you.

Parents never let anything stop them from taking care of their kids. Not even death."

Cassie dropped her gaze.

"You need a place to lie low." She walked out from behind the counter and Cassie took her in. She'd aged some in the last five years. A silver streak had grown into her dark hair and she had gained a little weight, but it wasn't anything too extreme. Cassie had no idea how old she really was. Her mom never spoke about it, but she was one of the wisest people Cassie knew.

"I don't know who to trust. I can't trust the Order of Fate, and I've burned all my contacts from work." Cassie picked up a purple ball and rolled it in her hand.

"You are on a path separate from where you were before," she said.

"I can't do this right now, Peggy. I can't get into my future."

"You're already there," Peggy said.

"I don't understand."

"You are a key, an oracle of sorts now. It won't change because you want it to," Peggy said.

"I didn't ask for this."

"No one does." Peggy waved towards the back of the store. "You can stay here for a while, but your path is going to take you to places you never thought you'd go."

"Let's just get through today before we talk about the future," Cassie said, glancing back at the windows. She could almost feel all the eyes focused on her. If they knew where she was, they might not stop at Peggy's wards, but she couldn't think about that. She just needed rest and a minute to breathe.

Cassie followed Peggy towards the back. There was a bed and some other items set up to make it seem more homey. Further down the hallway were the stairs that went upstairs to Peggy's apartment. She dropped her bag on the bed and sat beside it.

Peggy watched her and crossed her arms. Cassie caught her staring and shook her head. "Please don't do that."

"What?" scheme? said.

"Read me," Cassie said without looking away.

"Pfft, I'm not doing that." Peggy waved her hand at her.

"Right. You forget I've known you for a long time."

"You think you know me?" She turned to walk away when Cassie stopped her.

"Peggy, did you see what was going to happen to my mom?"

She stopped in her tracks and glanced back. "Some things have destiny written all over them."

8

Peggy

ew York 2005

PEGGY PACED HER STORE, waiting for some kind of word about what happened with Kat and the girls. She'd told Kat what was going to happen today. The way her daughter died, but something felt off. Her visions were almost always right. And if she was right today, her best friend would come home with one less child.

She walked to the back of her store and watched her daughter sleeping in the little bed she'd set up back there. She was so small and if anything threatened her, Peggy knew she would do the same as Kat. She'd try to get her as far from it as possible.

The girl moved slightly, and a red curl fell over her face. She was so small, and Peggy would do anything for her.

She heard the door to the shop open and went back to the front. Gareld was standing there watching her. His dark eyes filled with sadness.

"What happened?" Peggy demanded.

He shook his head. "Your vision… she changed it."

Peggy felt a wave of relief knowing Cassie was still alive, but Gareld's face didn't change.

"Peg, Kat's gone." He reached for her and pulled her into him. "She died saving Cassie."

Peggy felt herself go numb. Everything she'd been trying to prevent had still happened. The Demon. The warehouse. Everything is down to the moment of death. The only thing that had changed was who died.

"The girls can stay with me," Peggy said without hesitation.

"I'll bring them tonight. You know Cody is going to fight you on this."

Peggy pushed back from Gareld just enough to look into his eyes. "I don't care. They need someone that is going to take care of them. Not someone that is going to make them soldiers."

"Maybe that's what they need," Gareld said. "To learn to fight."

Peggy stared at him for a moment. "How can you say that? They're just children, only a few years older than Eli."

"I would hope Eli learns to fight, too. There are so many dangers out there that want to kill them. You know that better than anyone."

Peggy sighed. "At least give them time to grief. Then they can make their own choices."

Gareld pulled her back to him and Peggy let him hold her while she grieved her best friend and prepared herself for how things would change.

"I'm never telling anyone my visions again," she managed. "I will not be responsible for anyone else dying."

"You aren't the only one that knows what she is. There are others out there," Gareld said.

"Are they going to keep coming after her?" Peggy asked, not moving away from him.

"I hope not."

9

Cassie

Cassie heard voices and laid still, listening to them. One was clearly Peggy talking and pacing the hallway. Cassie couldn't make out the other right away. She rolled over and opened her eyes to see down the hallway towards Peggy's stairs. Sitting on the bottom step was Lark. Cassie sighed. Of course, she would know this would be the place to find her.

Lark's eyes met her, and she stood up. Cassie pulled herself to a sitting position on the bed and cocked her head.

"I knew you'd come here when you didn't get help from Cody," Lark said. "You know he means well."

"It doesn't take away what I know. He isn't what you think he is."

"I know what he is. He's a witch and has lived for a very long time," Lark said without a reaction.

"You knew?" Cassie said, shaking her head.

"Of course I knew. I didn't know the details, but I knew he's been at this for a long time.," she said.

"Did you know he knew the Vampires?"

"They weren't vampires then," she said.

Cassie walked into the storefront. "I don't care. Things change when your friends become evil."

"Are you sure you understand everything?" Lark said, following her.

"What's to understand? I don't hang out with demons."

"Mom, did."

Cassie stared at her. "You're lying."

"Why would I?" Lark said. "When Dad left, she went down a dark path with her magick. She turned to the only teachers she could find that didn't judge her for what she wanted to do."

Cassie shook her head.

"She was getting ready to be removed from the Order of Fate when she died. You don't remember any of this?" Lark took a step towards her and Cassie raised her hand.

"Stay back." Cassie didn't want anyone anywhere near her while she figured all of this out. She tried to remember, but she couldn't. None of this made any sense.

"Look, I'm not interested in taking you back to the Order. I just want you to be safe. We can get out of the city and the Vampires will find something else to occupy them, but Cody will not stop looking for you. He thinks he needs to protect whatever that book says."

"You want me to run?" Cassie was confused.

"I want you to live."

"You realize I have been on my own for a while," Cassie said again.

"Yeah, you keep reminding me. That doesn't mean you're safe now."

She glanced past Lark to Peggy. "What happens if I die?"

"What?" Lark said, looking from Cassie to Peggy.

"Does this thing go back in the box?"

"Do you pass the sight back to the book? Yes, but that won't be what happens."

Cassie bit her lip. "So, what happens?"

"You know I can't tell you that."

10

Cody

He closed the door and made his way across town. His old blue Mustang drove through downtown to the edge of the water. He knew Wesley would be waiting for him. He just didn't know if he would greet him or kill him.

He slammed the gear into park and waited. The surrounding darkness gave an odd look to the water and around his car. He'd seen a lot in the time he'd been alive, but he still got the chills from certain places. This was one of them.

He glanced up and saw a figure standing against a lamppost on the dock. He couldn't make them out, but knew it had to be Wesley. He palmed the wooden stake in his back pocket before opening his door and stepping out.

"You can't protect her," the figure said.

"I know, but I can keep you from killing her," Cody said.

"You did such a great job with Maggie." He raised his head and his eyes came into view.

Cody stopped and pulled his anger back. He wanted to keep a level head. "Cassie is off limits."

"No one said we were going to kill her. We need her." Wesley stepped into the light. His once young face looked aged. Which was odd for a vampire. Cody could see the restlessness in his eyes. "We're tired."

"You want to die?" Cody shook his head. "I don't believe you."

"You remember when this happened? Aren't you tired of fighting? We could end it all for both of us. All we have to do is to see who they are."

"I can't let you give this to someone else," Cody said.

"You can kill me, but Ami," He sighed. "You know she won't die. Would you rather have her as an enemy or a friend?"

"I can't keep working with you two. Too many know about our past. Too many are going to want me to stop fighting."

"So stop. Live your life and let me and Ami go," Wesley said. "You know you want to stop. We all do."

Cody swallowed hard. "Only if it ends for all of us."

"Deal."

* * *

NEW YORK 1903

Cody jumped out of the carriage and held out his hand. Maggie took it and stepped down. She still looked as beautiful as ever. She had decided since giving up the hunting to dress in clothing that didn't get her as noticed. She had on a beautiful pale purple dress with matching gloves. Cody loved she wanted to look good for their new home. The city was more than he expected, but when the governor of New

York wanted you to be his personal bodyguard, you answered. At least, that was what he figured.

"It's different here," Maggie said, "But I think we can still start our family in the city." She put her hand on her stomach.

Cody smiled, and they walked into their new townhome. It was large for New York and for him. He'd only known the desert and the little towns that dotted it.

"I think it will be. There is a lot to this town," Cody said. They had already set the furniture up in their new home and, for the first time, they had everything that made a home one.

"When do you work for the governor?" Maggie asked as she took a seat on the couch.

"Soon." Cody looked through the large picture window in the sitting room. "I still don't know how he heard about me."

Maggie shrugged. "You have been helping the sheriff on Superstition Mountain a lot. Word travels."

Cody said nothing. The truth was, he had no idea if that was why. He'd stopped hunting, but he did still help the locals with the occasional demon here and there. He wasn't about to let them hurt people he could help, and there was no way Wesley was going to worry about it. He was off living his life with Ami.

"I have to go get some things. Are you going to be okay?" He asked.

Maggie smiled and raised an eyebrow. "You know you aren't the only hunter that lives in this house?"

Cody turned and walked towards her. "I know, but it's good to be cautious. This is a new place with new people."

"I'll be fine," she said, and he nodded.

That was the last time Cody would see her alive.

11

Cassie

assie sat on the bed and shook her head. The voices of her sister and Peggy faded and she could hear her breathing in her ears. Her heart was beating hard in her chest. She closed her eyes and felt herself fall back.

The first thing she noticed was the soft grass tickling her ear. She let her eyes open and the sky above her took her by surprise. The surrounding air smelled of smoke and metal. She wasn't sure why it was, but she covered her nose and sat up. She choked on the smoke before pulling herself to her feet and taking in her surroundings.

She wasn't in the city, but she wasn't in a completely bare area, either. There were buildings all around her and one road ahead of her. The building to the left of her had rolling smoke and bits of fire poking from the window.

Cassie heard yelling in the distance towards the other side and swung her head in that direction. There were people running past her and screaming. She watched as fighter jets flew overhead and made a face. When she lowered her gaze, that wolf was standing in front of her. She eyed it and it shook its head. She watched in horror as its body bent at odd angles and the beautiful fur fell onto the ground, leaving a naked man breathing hard, with his head down. His light hair fell in front of his face. He glanced up and Cassie recognized the only feature that didn't change on a werewolf. His eyes.

"Why did you open the book?" He said, pushing himself to his feet.

Cassie looked away. "I didn't realize what would happen."

"You're a Witch. Don't they teach you about the book?"

Cassie snickered. "My teacher has a lot of secrets."

"You don't belong here," he said.

"I don't know how to control it," Cassie said simply. "I just want to give it back."

"That's not how it works." He circled her, still naked and not worried about it. She looked away, and he lowered his gaze. "You humans are so weird about nakedness."

"Why do I keep seeing you?" Cassie said, without missing a beat.

"You haven't figured that out?" He said.

She shook her head. "Of course. You're connected to the book." She made a face. "What am I supposed to do with you?"

"With me?" He asked, confused.

"Yeah, like how do I get you to go away?" She turned as she spoke and he was right there, so close she could feel the heat of his skin. She felt her breath catch and pushed it away.

"You can't." He stepped closer, and she took a step back. "Usually, it goes to a witch, Wolf Hybrid, but the universe thought it would do something weird this time, I guess."

"Hybrid?" She sighed and shrugged. "Sorry to disappoint. Where am I?"

"The future. I mean what it is right now?" He said looking around.

"Are you really here?"

"In a way. I'll still be alive when all this happens, it seems. At least right now," he said.

"Wait, what does that mean?"

"I'm Carik, by the way. In case you wanted to know," he said, holding out his hand. Cassie glanced at it before looking back at the chaos going on all around them.

"Do they not see us?"

"We're in between. Ghosts of the past that have the privilege of seeing the future."

"You think this is a privilege?" Cassie said. She shook her head. "I don't want to know any of this."

"But you have the chance to change it since you know what will happen. We were taught it's a great honor."

"You can take it back if you think it's such a great honor," Cassie said.

"That's not how it works."

"I don't want it," Cassie said, swinging her arms. "You hear me? I don't want it." She forced her eyes closed and shook her head. Everything spun around her. She felt dizzy and her stomach turned. When she opened her eyes, she was lying on the bed. Lark was sitting next to her, watching her.

"What did you see?" Peggy said from the other side of the room.

"Nothing really." Cassie held her arms over her chest. She hadn't processed what was going on, not really. She'd just started understanding everything that was going on with her and this book.

A knock at the shop door startled everyone. Peggy and Lark exchanged glances before she walked to the front, pulling the curtain closed behind her. Lark looked at Cassie and put her finger to her mouth, telling her to be quiet.

They could hear Peggy chatting with someone and then coming back through the curtain. She glanced at Cassie and crossed her arms. "It's for you."

Cassie stared at her. She didn't have any friends that would come here. No one knew about Peggy except her family. Cassie stood and walked into the storefront, with Lark following behind.

As soon as she locked eyes with him, she knew who he was. Carik.

"What are you doing here?" Cassie said, crossing her arms.

He glanced behind her and gave them a wave. "I'm Carik."

Lark didn't say anything and Cassie smiled. Good luck getting her to like you.

"I told you, I'm a protector of the book." He said.

"Then I'll give it to you," Cassie said, turning and walking back to the bed. She grabbed her bag and reached in to grab the book, but it was gone. Panic set in and she dug further.

Lark came up behind her. "Did you lose it?" she said.

"It's gone. I know I had it." Cassie sat on the bed and Carik came through the door into the little room. "You know, it's rude to come into a girl's bedroom uninvited."

He raised his eyebrows and crossed his arms. "The book isn't a physical thing anymore. It's you. You're the book."

"No, I'm not. I'm just a witch that steals magical artifacts and causes trouble for my sister. I'm not this thing." Cassie couldn't move. She couldn't think. There was no way she was this special thing. She'd never had this kind of responsibility and didn't want it.

"Sorry, sis, but it sounds like you are," Lark said. She turned to Carik. "What do we do now?"

"We have to get out of the city. Ami will be looking for her," Carik said.

"Wait, who's Ami?" Cassie shook her head. "Nevermind, I don't want to know."

He glanced at Cassie. "You can do this."

She glanced at Peggy, who shrugged. "This is your path."

"I don't run from things like this. I want to fight," Cassie said.

"You can't. If you go against her, you won't win," Carik said.

"She's just a Vampire. I've killed a lot of them."

"Not like her. She has the blood of the first demon now. She can't be killed."

"I can't run my whole life," Cassie said.

"No, but you can leave and learn how to use the power you have now. You have the ability to see everything that is coming at you before it happens."

Cassie stood. "And what happens to everyone here?" She liked to say she wasn't interested in keeping them safe, but she loved her sister.

"We'll get by. We can't let Cody know where you are, either. Not until we know what will happen." Lark put her hand on Cassie's shoulder. "What have you seen?"

Cassie dropped her gaze. "Nothing good. Just a lot of war and I don't know when it will happen."

"Is it soon?"

Cassie glanced at Carik. "I don't know."

"That's the kind of thing you need to learn," Carik said.

"What about Peggy? She can see the future," Cassie said, looking her way.

"It doesn't work on a wide scale. I only see the future of those I'm close to." Peggy shrugged as she spoke.

"You're important now. You have to learn how to use this in combination with your own witch gifts. You have to," Lark said. "I know I'm hard on you, but maybe mom knew in some way you would need to survive. Maybe that's why she did what she did."

Cassie stared at her sister. For the first time in a long time, she saw sadness and love at the same time. "What if she was wrong?"

"What if she wasn't?" Larks said, grabbing her hand. "You won't know unless you take this chance and do this. You have to. We have to know what to fight and how," Lark said.

Cassie plopped on the bed and thought about everything. Her whole world was crashing down around her. All she wanted was to go back to her life.

"It's your choice, but everyone who has used the book in the past has trained to use it. If you don't, you will be at its whim instead of controlling when you see things and what you see," Carik explained. "What do you want to do?"

"I'll go, but we have to get the training done quickly." She glanced at her sister. "I need to know about mom."

"You will as soon as you get back. I'll tell you everything."

* * *

CASSIE WATCHED the city fly by them as they made their way south. Carik wasn't saying much beyond telling her there was a pack where they were going and they'd be safe. Cassie thought about what wolves were to her. She'd never been around a pack before, only heard stories about them and how they'd been hunted down over the years. That was about all she knew.

"What's your pack like?" She didn't look at him as she spoke. "Should I be worried?"

"They're rough. They've been through a lot over the years." He glanced at her and then back to the road. "As far as being worried, not unless you intend to attack them."

Cassie looked at him, confused.

"They know how to deflect magick." He shrugged. "It comes from being interbred with witches at least once a generation."

"So, werewolves and witches are a thing?"

"Sometimes." He shrugged. "Mostly so we have someone that can handle the book. It was ours until someone stole it. This is the first time in centuries we've had it back in our hands."

"I'm not the book," Cassie snapped.

"You weren't, but now you are one with it. So, technically, you are the book."

Cassie looked out the window and watched the urban landscape turn slowly more rural. The trees became thicker, and the cars thinned out.

"It's not much further now," Carik said.

They'd been driving for a good part of the day, and Cassie was tired. She slowly felt herself drifting off until she opened her eyes and she was far from the car.

She watched as people were running around here. The ground was dry and dusty. She pulled herself together and watched as men in military uniforms motioned for a small group to follow. Cassie kept her eyes on a young woman and her daughter. The little girl wasn't over ten, with curly light brown hair and dark eyes. She was holding a stuffed black and white cow. The woman, her mother, was in obvious distress as she ran with her daughter being pulled behind her.

Cassie followed them as they made their way to what looked like an old military bunker. It was crowded and as everyone tried to file in, the woman realized there wasn't enough room. She glanced at the officer and handed her daughter to him. "Take care of her."

The child started to scream for her mother as she pushed the doors closed. The remaining group pounded on the metal door as the mother backed away, tears in her eyes. She turned to leave when she ran into what should have been a man, but was a twisted version with dark eyes and blood-soaked fingers. He smiled, letting his light hair fall into his face before he grabbed her and bit her.

Cassie startled awake, and Carik snapped his gaze to her. "What did you see?"

"Fucking Vampires."

* * *

Carik pulled the car into a garage on the left side of the road. By now, all the hints of the city were gone. They were in an area Cassie had never been before.

"What are we doing here?" She asked as he pulled the garage door down behind them. She could see the tools on the counter and an old mustang parked beside them. The back wheel was on a jack and the whole front of the once royal blue car was crushed. It had seen better days.

"This is my dad's shop. He won't mind us taking a break and getting some sleep." Carik opened the door to the receptionist area and motioned for her to go inside. The entire room was glass, but the blinds were pulled so no one could see inside. She took a seat on the couch before glancing back at him.

"I can't sleep. I'll get nothing but those future dreams," Cassie said with a shrug.

"It won't always be like that. You'll learn how to control it."

"When?" Cassie sighed and shook her head. "I made all the wrong choices in my life. I got my mom killed."

"Are you sure about that?"

"I was there. She died protecting me," Cassie said.

"Then she made a choice."

Cassie snapped her gaze to him. "What? No, she had to save me. She's my mom."

"Not every mom would die for their child." He shook his head. "You should at least try to get some sleep. Maybe you won't travel since you already did today."

"I don't know. I am tired, but it seems like the last 48 hrs. Have been nothing but seeing bits of a future I don't want."

"It will get easier." He put his hand on hers. Cassie let herself feel the warmth of his hand. It was comforting and made her feel like all of this was just a dream and she was warm in her bed and her mother was in the next room waiting for her to wake up. "I promise."

Cassie let herself smile and watched as Carik stood, his hand pulling away from her and all the safety going with it. She laid down and let herself relax.

Thankfully, there were no dreams, and she finally got some good sleep.

12

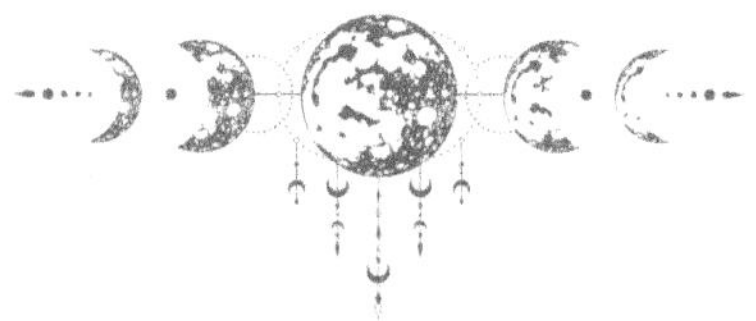

Carik

He stood at the garage door and watched her sleeping in the back of the car. She finally looked peaceful. He squared his jaw at the thought of her. He was not going to fall into the trap of caring for her. She was simply a part of his job.

He was the one to protect her and keep her safe, the one that was the book. The protector of the future. At least that was what the stories said.

She turned over, and he kept his eyes on her. He didn't realize he was holding his breath until he looked back out of the window.

He couldn't deny the way he'd felt when his eyes had met hers. The pull to protect her and keep her from any harm that might come her way.

And he hated it.

As the sun rose, he decided it was time to wake her up and finish getting to his home. He sighed as he walked to her and hit the side of the car.

"It's time to go," he said.

She startled awake, and he immediately felt a tinge of regret at being so pushy.

She sat up and rubbed her eyes and he tried to ignore the fact she was moving so slowly. He was there to protect her, not wait for her like a servant, even though he knew he'd do anything she asked.

"What's going on?" She asked.

"You ask that a lot," he said as he pulled the garage door open. "We still have a couple of hours to go."

She slid out of the back of the car and stretched.

He stood by the driver's door and watched her. Her light hair was messy and loose, even though she'd put it in a ponytail before she went to sleep. He caught himself thinking about pushing the strand that was falling in her face behind her ear.

"What are you smiling about?" she said.

He quickly dropped the smile and opened the door to the driver's side and got in. She did the same on the passenger side and he fired up the car.

Once they were outside the garage, he got out and pulled the door down. The shop was in the middle of nowhere, but he wasn't going to leave it open for everyone to go into.

Once he got back in the car, he glanced at Cassie. She had curled her legs up into her lap and was leaning on the door, clearly still tired.

"You can sleep on the way," he said.

She glanced at him and rolled her eyes. "I realize that, but I might have one of those future things."

"You mean where you see everything that's coming?" He let a slight laugh slip out.

"It's not funny. It's scary," she said and pulled her knees

closer to her chest.

He sighed and nodded. "It is scary, but that's why you see it, so you can change it."

"Peggy says you can't change things. They always happen."

He shrugged, "maybe."

"Wait, you're in the visions, too. Do you remember what you see?"

He swallowed hard. He didn't know how much he should tell her. "I remember everything I see when I'm with you." He felt like that was simple, but also explained everything she needed to know.

"How come you're there?"

"It's part of the way the book works. The one meant to use it sees everything. The protector sees what she does," he said. "It only works for you. You can control it."

"I can't," she said.

"That's why we're going to my home. It's where the book was made."

"I don't understand," she said.

"My pack has been the protector of that book since we can remember." He sighed. "When it was stolen from us, we searched for it, but we couldn't find it. There was no signature, no protector until it was found and activated."

"So, when I found it, you did too?"

He nodded. "I did, and I found you."

They rode in silence until they came to the small town just north of the Georgia border. It was just as he remembered it. The streets were lined with parked cars and the houses looked like they always did. All but his old home. But they weren't going there, thankfully.

13

Lark

New York 2005

Lark walked through Peggy's shop door, holding Cassie's hand. She couldn't think or breathe. She'd just watched her mother die and there was nothing she could do. Everything was upside down.

Peggy rushed to her and pulled her and Cassie into her arms. Lark melted into her and let everything go. She felt exhausted and confused and she didn't want to do anything but lay down with her mother and never wake up. But that wasn't an option. She had a sister to look out for and people that needed her. No matter what was happening with her.

"You both can stay here for as long as you want," Peggy said.

Lark pulled back from Peggy. "I don't want to stay here."

Peggy looked at her, confused.

"I want to go back to the Order," Lark said. "Cassie should stay. She needs someone."

Peggy smiled. "Stay a few days and we will talk about it after."

"No, I need to do this now," Lark said. "Take me back to the Order."

"You don't want this. You're hurting," Peggy said.

"No, I have to learn everything I can, so this never happens to anyone I love again," Lark said, fighting back tears. "That's all that's left for me now."

"No, it's not. We're here for you and always will be," Cassie said. Her little face was red from crying. She grabbed her sister's hand and pulled her to her. Lark wanted to fight them and leave, but she didn't. Her sister was right. They all had to look after each other now. No matter what.

14

Cassie

"This is it, my home," Carik said with a huge smile on his face. It was clear to Cassie he was happy about being back here, even if the circumstances weren't great.

Cassie took in the small town around her. She hadn't even realized they were close to anything. When Carik had woken her this morning, she thought they'd get something to eat or spend a little more time in the car, but less than four hours later they were parking in front of a large farmhouse with dogs running at the car barking.

She waited for Carik to get out first, and the smile on his face as he petted the two brown and white boxers that jumped at him told her everything. He might seem like the big bad wolf, but he was just like her and they were both in this mess together. That gave her a little comfort.

"Carik? What are you doing here?" A woman who looked to be about fifty said as she pushed the old screen door open. Cassie took her in and she was not what she expected. The woman looked normal, with dark blonde hair with wisps of silver throughout. She glanced back at Cassie. "Who's this?"

"She's someone that needs help," Carik said.

"She's not one of us," she said.

"She's bonded with the book, Shirley."

Shirley slid her gaze to Cassie and shook her head. "How is that possible?"

Carik shrugged. "I don't know, but it did."

She sighed and motioned for them to follow her.

Cassie walked behind Shirley and Carik up the walkway onto the large wrap-around porch and through her front door. The living room was large, with an old couch sitting against the far wall. There was a small table on the other side. She motioned for Cassie to sit on the couch and Carik leaned on the wall in the corner. Shirley sat in the chair across from her.

"So, I'd really like to know how this happened. The way it goes is usually a hybrid of witch and wolf. You are clearly not a wolf." She sat back and took Cassie in. "Why just a witch?"

Cassie shrugged. "I don't know. I just picked it up and everything changed."

"This is unusual. I'm guessing you want us to help her?" She glanced at Carik as she spoke.

"We don't have much of a choice. She's still got to navigate the future and help us figure out what is coming," he said.

"It has to be big if this has happened," she said.

"Not to put a kink in things, but how are you going to help me?" Cassie leaned back on the couch.

"If you haven't noticed, wolves have a connection to the book."

"Yeah, I have," Cassie said.

"This is going to be a crash course," Shirley said.

"Where do we start?"

* * *

"I DON'T UNDERSTAND what we're doing?" Cassie stood in the center of the room, watching the others.

"The idea is to start with something small. You need to control when you are connecting to the energy of the book. This way, you will be able to use it when you want to."

"How is this helpful?"

"If you can see the future a few minutes ahead, then you'll know what is going to happen and can shape it," Carik said.

Cassie turned and shook her head. "It only happens when I fall asleep."

"That's what we want to change," Shirley said. "Try connecting when you are awake. More of a meditation rather than actually being fully asleep."

Carik grabbed her shoulders gently. "Close your eyes."

She did as she was told.

"See yourself standing with the book."

Cassie let her mind relax and the book was sitting in front of her in a dark room. There was no one there. No one asking her to do things or wondering about what her next move was. She was alone with a book that could tell her everything about the future. It was nice and peaceful.

She took a step towards it and put her hand on it. The heat coming from it spread through her body. It warmed as she connected with it. Her body felt like it was on fire and then she was standing there, in the middle of a burning building where the house once stood. She walked through the building to the other side of the door and down into the street. All the buildings were on fire. She covered her mouth to keep the ash from getting into her lungs. The smell of burning wood filled her nose. She tried to see when this was happening, but everything looked as though it had been through a war. While she'd connected differently, she was still too far in the future for what they wanted. At least she'd figured out how to connect without going to sleep. At least she hoped she had.

She closed her eyes and let herself drift to the darkroom. Her hand was still on the book and she pulled it back slowly, letting herself drift back to the present. Cassie opened her eyes, and she was still on her feet in the center of the room.

"What did you see?" Shirley asked as soon as her eyes were open.

Cassie swallowed hard. How do you tell someone their house is gone in the future? She sighed and smiled before she realized she just couldn't. "The same old war stuff."

Carik caught her gaze and knew there was more to it, but didn't say anything. "Great, so you have that, at least."

"Does that mean I can actually sleep without the interruptions?"

"I don't know."

"I thought you guys had done this before?" Cassie sat on the edge of the couch. Just that small session had been a lot for her.

"I haven't," Carik said. "The book has been lost for a long time. We are going off what we have been told."

"That makes me feel better," she said sarcastically.

"We will figure it out. It seems we are on the right track

already," Carik smiled as he spoke. "Soon you will be able to drop in and out of the future at a moment's notice."

Cassie smiled. She knew what they wanted, but she wasn't sure she was going to be able to do it. It seemed so hard and there was no time. Lark and the others were still dealing with the Vampires and Demons that were now looking for her. She knew they wouldn't be safe anywhere.

"Let's go again," she said.

15

Ami

Ami pulled herself from the safety of her room and went into the main part of the building they were living in. It was old and falling in, but that never bothered her. It was the age of the building that she loved. The structure was built in the late 1800s and reminded her of when she was younger. When she actually knew what she was fighting for. She'd been the hero once, fighting for those that needed help, but evil never dies and she was now that evil living in the world with the humans. Things had changed so much. She knew that now more than anyone.

"What are you doing out here, my love?" Wesley said as he walked through the door. The noise of the city outside buzzed in her ears. Even though it was early morning, people were out doing their things and creating their lives. She was stuck in this coffin of sorts she couldn't escape. The busy world was just too much for her.

"I can't stay in that room any longer. Did you find the book?"

Wesley shook his head. "I don't know what they did with it, but I'll find it and we will figure out how to transfer this so you can be free. Did your informant know anything?"

"Just that the girl and the book left the Order of Fate." She sighed.

"You will be free," he said.

"We will be free," she corrected.

The sound of the door opening caught her off guard and she snapped her head towards a demon walking into the room. Wesley turned and put his body in front of Ami and eyed the Demon.

"Relax, I have news," the Demon leaned on the wall and crossed his arms.

"How would you know anything more than I do?" Wesley asked with a smile. He cocked his head and stared at him.

The Demon met his gaze and raised an eyebrow. "Okay, if you don't want to believe me, then I could just leave."

Ami stepped in front of Wesley and smiled. "Of course not. If you have news, please share it."

The Demon glanced at Wesley and smiled before taking a step forward. "Cassie Storm is who you are looking for."

Ami glanced at Wesley before looking back to the Demon. "Are you sure? That's a very interesting name."

Ami smiled, but didn't let on. She already had that information. The less the others working for her knew, the better.

"Yep, talked to her myself," The Demon said.

"You're a water demon, right?" Ami smiled as she spoke. "Do you have a name?"

"Pycot," he said without missing a beat..

"You've been around for a while, haven't you?"

"Not as long as you, but yes," he said.

"Why haven't I worked with you before?"

"We stay to ourselves normally," he said.

"But not you."

"I've broken from my clan. We had a difference of opinion," he said simply.

Ami walked closer to him and let her hand land on his chest. "I think we could work together to find her and to bring her here." She let her fingers trace his collar and smiled. "Aren't there two sisters in that family?"

"Yes, but she's with the Order of Fate. There's no way to get in there."

"They have to leave the Order from time to time. Bring her to me and I'll make sure you are rewarded more than you ever thought you could be without a clan."

Pycot bit his lip before nodding and glancing at her hand. "Whatever you desire."

Ami smiled and cocked her head. She'd seen the Demons that wondered the world and hunted them just like Cody and his Order. When it started, she'd been one of the first to join. The memories ran through her like ice water and she shook them away.

Pycot took this as his opportunity to bow and leave.

Wesley watched her. "Where were you just now?"

She glanced at him and forced a smile. "I remembered the past. You remember when we met?"

"Of course. You were an annoying girl who wanted to conquer the world. It was my job to protect you."

"It was your job to teach me," she corrected.

"I failed you then. I let Price turn you into what you are now. I should have stopped it."

"You tried, but sometimes fate has other plans."

16

Cassie

Cassie found herself standing in the middle of the city. Everything was standing, and wood, it still had the same weird smells. The sound of traffic and yelling made her smile. Maybe this time she hadn't gone so far ahead. She walked out into the street so she could see where she was.

She was less than a block from her home. She walked towards it and saw her apartment still standing at the top of the stairs. She climbed the steps and stopped outside of the door. It looked fine, but she wasn't sure. She let her hand run down the wood, taking in the feeling of it.

Her wards weren't up and it was cold. Her hand rested on the nod for a moment before she turned it and walked inside. The place looked totally different. The living room that she had kept her whole life in was clean, with wood floors and white walls. She took it in and bit her lip. It felt like she was breaking into someone's house and spying on them. She kind of was, but didn't want to think about that idea.

A young girl walked into the kitchen and sat at the table. She had light hair and wasn't over ten years old. Her back was to Cassie, but the air had gotten thick with her presence. This girl was a witch.

Cassie stepped back and waited, but nothing happened and she felt herself falling again and knew she was coming out of the book. She opened her eyes and was sitting in her bed. The darkness was all around her.

The breeze flowed through the open window, blowing her hair from her face. She stood and walked to the window, unsure of what she would see. She hadn't wasted any time getting herself in the bed and resting. It had been days since she'd been able to really have a moment to herself. It was all about training and learning how to go in and out of the future. One thing Cassie hadn't tried was going into the past. A part of her wondered if she could and if she would see her mother. She leaned on the wall and peered down at the street. It was bare and there were very few people in this little place. Cassie thought about how peaceful it must have been growing up here and what she could have had if she hadn't been in a different place if she wouldn't have lived like she did. Maybe her mother would still be here.

Cassie pulled her sleep pants on and opened her door. She made her way towards the stairs and down to the kitchen. Voices made her stop in her tracks.

"Why did you bring her here?" Shirley's voice carried through the small hallway.

"You know why?" Carik answered.

"She's an outsider. Even if she can help us, why would she?"

"She's part of the Order of Fate," Carik said.

"All the more reason to get her out of here before anyone else realizes who she is," Shirley said with a sigh. "Look, we've helped her kind before and it always blows up in our faces. The treaty is long over. They won't accept her here."

"They don't have to. They just have to let me finish the training. Then we're going back. I need her to be safe," Carik said.

"What is it with you and her?"

"Nothing. I'm just fulfilling my duty," Carik said before moving further away. She couldn't hear what he said next. Cassie strained to listen, but all she heard was her own heart beating in her chest. *What do they know that I don't?*

"You can come in now," Shirley's voice echoed up the hall.

Cassie bit her lip like she was a child that had gotten caught listening to her parents fight. She decided to show herself and find out what exactly they were talking about. "What are you talking about?"

"You, but something tells me you already know that," Carik said with a half smile.

"Why am I such a threat?"

"We haven't had a witch here for several generations. We used to be the largest pack in the northern United States. We made a deal with a witch to help keep our lines safe." Shirley said.

"It went bad. The pack was almost destroyed," Carik finished for her.

"When we rebuilt what we could, we made a deal not to have a witch here again. We have to protect our legacy," Shirley said, taking a drink of her tea.

"I'm not here to do any harm to you or your people. I just came to learn," Cassie said, without thinking. "I didn't want to come, but I don't know how I can beat someone who is so powerful."

"The Vampire leader. She's not like any other vampire we've seen," Carik said.

"All the more reason to get this done with and get you out of here," Shirley remarked.

"I agree. I'm trying to get to my family. I want to keep them safe. I can't do that if I can't see what's coming."

"You're almost there," Shirley said. She glanced at Carik.

"What aren't you telling me?" Cassie said, without missing a beat.

"I'm going with you when you leave." Carik said with a smile.

"But what about your family?"

"I don't have one. I've been in the city for a long time."

Cassie nodded her head. "Okay, but if you are coming with me, we need a few ground rules."

"Can't wait." He stood. "Let's get back to work."

17

Lark

Lark watched as Cody walked to the building through her window. She had a feeling there was something really wrong with what was going on. She hadn't told him about where Cassie had gone and why, but she figured he would find out anyway at some point.

She watched his face as he looked like he was bothered by something. Had he already found out? She had to know. Lark walked down the stairs and met him in the hallway before his office. He looked worn and tired, like he'd done something he would regret.

"What happened?" She asked.

"I just went hunting." He rubbed the back of his neck. "Did you find your sister?"

"No," she lied.

"That's a shame. I was hoping she could give me some insight into how this all might end for all of us." He walked past her and opened his office door. "What can we do?"

"I don't know. She usually comes back when she feels

like it. Sometimes that's a day or two and other times that's months before anything happens."

"How long do you think it will be?"

"You seem awfully concerned about how long she's going to be gone. Is there something else going on?" Lark followed him into his office and sat in the chair across from his desk.

He looked at her, his age finally showing in his eyes. She knew he was old, but until yesterday, she had no idea how old.

"I just want to get Ami and Wesley out of the city."

"And Cassie can do that?" Lark asked.

"I know she can. She just has to give them the book."

"I thought that wasn't possible," she said.

"There may be a way." He looked down as he spoke. "Where is she?"

"I don't know. I didn't see her again after you and her spoke. What do you mean there might be a way? Will she be okay if the book is taken?"

"You mean after we had that fight?" He shook his head. "She doesn't know what is at stake." He sighed. "If what I've been told is true, then yes."

"Is it that, or are you trying to make sure your past doesn't come back to haunt you?"

He sat at his desk and Lark closed the door behind her. "Does anyone else know about your relationship with Wes and Ami?"

"No. Everyone is dead."

"And yet you're still alive. How is that possible?" Lark cocked her head and narrowed her eyes. She'd never dared to ask it, but if what she was thinking was right, her sister was in more danger than she'd ever been before.

"There are things you don't know about. People have different ways of navigating this world."

"That doesn't answer my question."

He watched her.

Lark didn't move. She crossed her arms in front of her. This was important, and she had to protect her family.

"Tell me how you did it."

"Did what?"

"Lived this long."

He bit his lip. "A friend helped me."

"That doesn't make any sense," Lark pressed.

"I have a lot of friends you don't know about with powers that no one has seen before and probably never will again. My friend saved me from my own death. This was the consequence."

"So, you're immortal,"

"Not exactly." Cody sighed and shook his head. "I was just given a longer life than most. It's already wearing off. Before long, I'll be dead and gone, and the Order of Fate will be left to someone else.

"Were you there when it started, the Order I mean?" Lark wasn't going to stop asking questions now. She'd never been able to get him to open up like this before.

"No." Cody didn't go into detail, but Lark could see something in what wasn't said.

"What do you need?"

18

Cassie

Cassie tiptoed down the hallway into the kitchen. The last time she's snuck down here, they were talking about her and why they wanted her to leave. She was so over the drama of werewolves and witches. Didn't they know a whole world was at stake? She'd seen a war, and they wanted her to concentrate on the near future. Maybe she should just leave. No one wanted her there, not really, and she's learned enough to fall into the book on her own. She didn't need a werewolf slowing her down.

She'd managed not to wake up the others, which was amazing considering what they were. She opened the fridge and took out the pitcher of sweet tea she'd watched Shirley make earlier that day.

Cassie sat it on the counter and took a glass from the cupboard. It was nice to have a break from the work she'd been doing., but it was paying off. The last few weeks she'd learned to put herself in the timeline closer to where they were actually living. She was understanding this weird new thing she had and how it made her different.

Cassie took a sip of her tea and sighed. Everything was confusing. She'd known about Werewolves and Vampires and Demons her whole life, but the Order of Fate didn't see them as different from each other. She was seeing some of the flaws in how the Order worked. Maybe it wasn't such a bad thing she left when her mom died. Even if that wasn't the reason behind it.

She put the pitcher back in the fridge and carried the glass towards the stairs. A spark of movement made her stop and look into the dark living room. She sat the glass down on the hallway table and stepped slowly into the darkness, letting herself feel the room with her energy. The first thing he noticed was the unique feeling of the Werewolves magick. It wasn't like hers, but it wasn't too different either. It felt strange as it pulled at her, but hauntingly familiar. The movement slammed against the magick and she put her guard up just before it slammed into her, knocking her to the ground.

The wolf was small. Probably half of the size of Carik when he was in wolf form. It growled at her and kept its dark eyes fixed on her. Cassie pushed it off without a lot of trouble and pulled herself to her feet. The wolf growled and took a step towards her.

"Hey, I'm on your side," Cassie pleaded.

The wolf answered with another bark and a low and growl. He wasn't listening to anything she had to say. He just wanted to kill her and sort out the rest later. At least that was the feeling she was getting from all the growling and attacking.

"Really, I don't know what you want from me," she stood still, and the wolf eyed her before it backed away.

It shifted into a human and put his hand on the back of the couch. Cassie stood still, watching what was going on in front of her. He pulled himself to his feet and his dark eyes met hers.

"So, you're the Witch that's supposed to help us." He shook his head and sighed. "You can't even do anything against a wolf."

"I didn't want to hurt you," Cassie said.

He snickered.

"What are you even doing here?" She said, not taking her eyes off of him.

"I wanted to see for myself," he said. He didn't move, and neither did she.

"They were trying to keep it under wraps. Guess that didn't work," she said.

"Nothing stays secret here." He glanced down at his naked body and gave a wicked smile. "Do you have a blanket or something?"

"What, you didn't think about clothes before you came over here to start trouble?"

He cocked his head. "Well, I could just walk out," he said as he started walking towards her.

She put her hands up and turned away. "There's a blanket on the back of the couch."

She heard him grab it. "I'm Kierin, by the way. Who are you?"

Cassie turned back towards him and shook her head. "Why should I tell you anything?"

"You don't have to. I'll just find out from my brother. He can't keep a secret."

"Your brother?" She cocked her head, and he gave her another wicked smile.

"Yes, Carik is my little brother. You can't tell?"

Cassie gave him a dirty luck, but she honestly didn't know what to think of all that. Of course, he had family. Why did he lie to her?

"I'll leave you to whatever you were doing, but you're going to have to come out to the rest of the wolves or they are going to wonder about why you're here. Trust me, they can feel you."

Fantastic.

* * *

SHE SIGHED as she tried to connect to the book again. She closed her eyes and reached for it in her mind. The book seemed to push back into the darkness. It was fighting against her. She pushed into the energy of the book and it slammed shut in front of her.

She shook her head and opened her eyes. "I can't do this. It won't let me connect."

"Try harder," Shirley said, standing over her. "This is how it works. You push into the book and it shows you what you need to see."

Cassie looked at her. "I'm not even connecting with it today. I have done nothing but trying to connect to this book, but it's just not happening."

"If you don't do it now, you won't be able to do it in time to change anything," Shirley said.

This caught Cassie's attention. "What are you talking about?"

"Nothing," she muttered and stood. "Do it again."

Cassie jumped up. "If you can't be honest with me and

tell me everything you know, I'm not doing this with you today."

Cassie stormed out of the room and through the kitchen. She didn't know where she was going, but standing in the kitchen was Carik, holding a drink. He watched her for a moment.

"What?" she said.

"Nothing, you're just not trying." He said, taking a drink of his sweet tea.

"I'm not trying?" She seethed. "You have no idea what i's like."

Cassie glared at him as he casually shrugged and walked into the garage. Rage filled her as she stormed after him.

"You think this is easy?" she demanded.

"No, I don't think it is. That is why I brought you here." He said, keeping his back to her.

"You have no clue how hard this is." She grabbed his shoulder and yanked him around. His eyes sharpened for only a second before she realized what was happening. His lips were on her so quick. Pressing his tongue into her mouth until she opened up for him.

He pulled her into him so hard she dissolved into him when she felt her back slam into the workbench. His hands squeezing her ass, pulling her onto the bench. For a minute he pulled back, keeping eyes on her. Waiting for the consent she eagerly gave.

She knew in that moment she needed to feel something, and he was the perfect one to feel it with. She didn't want to admit it to herself, but she felt something for him.

He unbuckled her belt. In one motion, he yanked it off her. She felt the slight burn of friction. He wrapped the belt around her hands in one motion. She gasped as his lips crashed into hers. Gripping the belt part in the middle, he pushed her against the wall, while his other hand pulled at her pants. He slid them from her body and threw them to the ground.

She closed her eyes and threw her head back. She wanted him not just today, but for the long haul. He had given everything to her and she was still fighting him. She didn't want to fight him anymore; she wanted everything he had and everything he was.

He undid his own pants in one motion and rubbed the head of his cock against her. Rocking his hips so the tip was barely touching her. She pushed forward with need, and he pushed her back against the wall. Her ass was sitting on the workbench at the perfect height. All she needed to do was rock forward just a little, and she would have everything she needed in that moment.

His hand slipped between her legs, and his thumb brushed against her throbbing clit. She let out a gasp as he bit her lip.

"You're not the one in control here, sweetheart," he growled as he pulled his hand back just a little. She moaned as he pulled his hand away and leaned back.

Carik grabbed her hands and held them against the wall with one hand as he pulled at her shirt with the other. He pulled it over her head and arms and threw it to the ground. She arched back as his mouth kissed the groove between her breasts. He pulled her bra off and threw it on top of her clothes. She watched him through slitted eyes as he stood there looking at her with a smile on his face.

"What?" she managed between waves of want.

"You're so fucking beautiful," he said as he closed the distance and pulled her against him. The full body of his cock rubbed her pussy, and she whimpered. He kissed her hard, and she tried to pull her hands free, but he pushed them against the wall again and she rocked her hips.

She gave a small gasp as he entered her. Wrapping his arm around her hips, he pushed against her pussy and she cried out. He quieted her with his mouth. Her gasping came quick as he covered her mouth with his. She moaned when he ground his pelvic into her as he drove harder and harder. Cassie couldn't keep thoughts in her head. She'd never wanted anyone like this and he was hers, all hers.

Her body shuttered, and she felt herself release against his cock. He pulled her hard into him as he thrust hard. She felt her legs go numb, and he slowly released her hands. She kissed him back deeply, tasting every part of his lips. He stood there holding her and looking into her eyes before he pulled out of her only long enough to flip her around.

Pressing her down on the table, he used one of his legs to kick hers up to the low stool. He teased her clit with the tip of his cock and her breath caught. He slid into her and she moaned. Her entire world had changed, but now, in this moment, she only felt the pleasure that this man, this Wolf, was giving to her and she didn't want it to stop.

He grabbed her hips, pulling her into him as hard as he could as he slid into her.

She grabbed the edge of the table with her bound hands and pushed against him to meet each thrust. She closed her eyes as she felt herself peaking again, just in time for him to stop. He pulled her hair, and she arched into him.

"I want you to beg for it," he whispered in her ear.

Cassie couldn't form words. She moaned in response.

"Say it."

She took a breath as he moved inside her. "Please," she managed.

"What?" He said.

She could hear the smile in his voice. He was enjoying this. "Please, fuck me."

He didn't let go of her hair as he pounded into her. She held the edge of the table and gasped as she felt the orgasm roll through her. She couldn't control herself and moaned loudly. He reached around and put his hand over her mouth.

"Shhh," He said between thrusts until they both peaked. He rested gently against her. He let her go, but stayed inside her for a few moments.

Her legs were shaking and could barely hold her up, so she was thankful he hadn't moved yet.

He slowly pulled away and grabbed his pants. "Next time, it won't be in a garage," he teased.

The movement inside the house made them both spring into action, putting on clothes just in time before Shirley opened the garage door. She looked at both of them and sighed. "Time to get back at it"

19

Lark

She walked down the hallway, thinking about what had just happened. Should she give up her sister to Cody? Even with everything going on, she wasn't sure that was the right call. He'd lied to them about who he was and she didn't know if she could trust anything he said.

She made her way through the door at the end of the hallway and headed for her room. The last thing she wanted was to be out here in the hall in her thoughts.

She opened her door and closed it behind her, letting the worry about what would happen next settle over her. She knew this wasn't what she wanted, but if he really could take the book out of her sister, it was worth a try, right?

Lark bit her lip and sighed. She let her gaze slide to the picture of her mother. She'd know what to do. It was a shame she wasn't here to help her figure it out.

"What do I do, mom?" Lark let her finger trail over the picture and a smile came to her face. She closed her eyes and flashes of the worst day of her life came to her mind.

The day her mother died.

* * *

Lark slammed against the wall behind her. Her breath was hard and the sting of pain in her ankle made her flinch. She glanced to her left. The warehouse was larger than they'd thought, and three people were not enough to stop these demons. Lark glanced at the one that had just thrown her. A tall, putrid looking thing. Its skin was slimy and green. Its eyes blinked like a snake, but its body was undeniably human looking. It shouldn't be possible, but here it was. Standing right in front of her.

"You Witch think you're better than everyone else, but you have no idea what you have done," it hissed at her.

"What are you even talking about?" Lark said, letting her hand slide behind her back. She grabbed the small ball she'd slid into her pocket before they'd come on the mission.

"Your mother didn't tell you everything. But why would she?" It laughed as it started to bring its hand down on her. Lark quickly pulled the cold ball from behind her back. She whispered a spell under her breath and let it fly, hitting the Demon in the chest.

It recoiled in pain before it froze from the spot in its chest all the way up its body. The ice curling like tendrils of icicles until it was completely covered.

Lark pulled herself to her feet even through the pain and closed her eyes. She searched for her mother with her magick until she felt her and hurried her away.

She was standing in front of Cassie with her hand up.

This Demon shook its head and then looked at Cassie before laughing. Her mother said a spell, and the Demon backed away before exploding into a gob of flying goo.

She glanced at Cassie and then at Lark. Lark could feel the relief in the fact they were both alive wash over her before something dropped from the top of the warehouse. It fell in front of her mother and their eyes locked before she put her hand out and Cassie slid across the floor.

Lark and her mother held each other's gaze for what seemed like forever, waiting for what was next. Even though it was just a few seconds.

Then everything exploded.

Protect your sister.

* * *

Lark took a huge breath in as she realized where she was. She was in her room, safe and not there anymore. She bit her lip.

"What was that?" She put the picture down and let herself lay in her bed. Tomorrow she had a lot to do and getting her sister back was high on that list. Getting the book out of her would save her. She knew it.

20

Cassie

"I'm so tired of this," she said as she fell into the chair. "I can't keep going into the future when I have no idea what I'm looking at."

"That's how it starts. Soon you'll just know what is going to happen without going in," Carik said.

"Sure," she glanced around her. "If I can survive the wolves here."

He made a face. "I'm guessing you're talking about my brother."

"Yeah, you couldn't tell me about him?"

"Why would I?" He shook his head. "None of the others are supposed to know you're here."

"Well, they do and I would have liked a heads up. Why would you lie about your family?." She let her head fall back and looked at the ceiling.

"I didn't want there to be any complications."

"Complications. Oh, there are so many complications.

Why can't I just figure this out and get back home?know, My sister needs me."

"You know people who carry this usually train their whole lives. You're getting a crash course," Carik said, sitting down across from her. He sighed. "What if we skipped training today?"

She raised her head and cocked an eyebrow. "Can we? I'd love a break."

He smiled. "Sure, but you have to come with me somewhere special."

She nodded, happy with a chance to let her brain rest. The whole last couple of weeks were nothing but trying to get her new powers to show her how to avoid things being thrown at her. She had the bruises to show it wasn't working.

They walked for what seemed like forever. The hills rolled before them and then turned into the forest. It was an amazing feeling. The energy in this place was more than she'd felt in a long time. The city teemed with its own kind of energy, but it was fueled more by people. This was purely nature based. It was beautiful.

"This was a sacred site for wolves. We came here to give thanks to the ancestors before us and to ask for their help." Carik smiled as he touched one of the stones in front of them.

Cassie glanced around her and realized they were standing in the middle of a circle of sorts. The same way witches would cast their own circle for rituals. The wolves were doing the same in their own ways.

"This is where they did the training of those like you," he said. "It was supposed to help focus power."

"Then why have we been training in the house?" Cassie watched him as she spoke. It made sense to her that they would want her power to be focused, but they weren't doing everything they could, which was odd to her.

"Because it's long since lost its power. As part of the agreement, years ago, the witches would power the circle to contain the power. That hasn't happened in a very long time."

"There's still power here. I can feel it. It's not the same as what I feel in the city, but it's here." Cassie raised her hands as she spoke and a wind kicked up.

"I thought your power came from you."

"It does, but it also comes from around us. Places like this don't lose their power. It just sometimes changes." She smiled at him.

"Do you want to try again?"

"Here?" Cassie said.

He nodded, and she shrugged. Cassie closed her eyes and let her mind wonder. There was so much here that she could hold. The energy from the trees or even the earth itself had a beat to it. Almost as though they were giving her a gentle hug and telling her they were there to help. She tapped into it and let her mind travel. She thought about her sister and was instantly there with her as she was standing in an alley. She had a box in her hand with ornate decorations on it. She was facing towards her with tears running down her face.

"You can't do this to us. I won't let you," she said.

"You have no control over the future," a voice said behind Cassie. It made her shiver, and she held her breath as she turned to face it. Cassie looked up and saw only a mass of dark, swirling energy. It moved with purpose as it closed the gap between it and her sister. The scream her sister let out broke Cassie's heart. It ripped the box from her hand and she fell to the ground. A deep wound across her neck.

Cassie stepped back before she realized she had just watched her sister die and there was nothing she could do from this point of view, but this was the future and she only needed to know when it happened to stop it. Finally, something she could use. But it was the worst thing she'd experienced since her mother.

Cassie pulled herself to her body. Carik was holding her up. He looked at her with concern in his eyes. "What did you see?"

"I have to get back to the city now."

"That could be a problem," a voice said behind her. Cassie turned to see that damn water demon standing at the edge of the circle. "If you go back to the city, Ami will kill you."

"If I don't go, my sister will die," Cassie snapped.

"Better her than you."

Cassie took a step towards him. "You don't belong here."

"Nope, yet here I am, giving you a warning instead of taking you right to her," he said.

"Why," Carik interrupted, stepping between Cassie and the Demon.

He slid his gaze towards him and smiled. "I have my reasons."

"I don't doubt that, but I still don't trust you," Cassie said.

He shrugged. "Call it an owed favor."

"I don't owe demons any favors," Cassie said with disdain in her voice.

"Who said it was a favor to you?" He raised an eyebrow and laughed slightly. "Stay out of the city if you want to live.

Don't if you want to die. I really don't care." Before Cassie could say anything else, he was gone.

"I don't care what that Demon says, I'm going back. Mys sister needs me."

"Maybe, but I think she can take care of herself," Carik said with a slight smile.

Cassie gave him a look. "You have no idea what you're talking about." She knew her sister and what they'd been through together, how she protected her when their mother died.

"I can't let her die."

21

Lark

She followed Cody to the edge of the city before he pulled his old car over and looked her way. "You're not stalling me, are you?"

She hesitated. "I was going to, but I want this book out of Cassie as much as you want to be done with these vampires."

"You don't know how happy I am that you said that," Cody smiled and sighed. "Look, if we can get Cassie back to them, then they can take what they need and she will survive."

"Then what?" Lark asked.

"Then the treaty is over and we'll go to war," Cody answered. He turned to Lark and shook his head. "It's the price of saving her."

"Why would you risk war with them when you don't have to?"

"It was always coming. I didn't see it. I only saw them as

who they were, but they aren't who they used to be. They were my friends," Cody said.

"Now, they're monsters," Lark finished for him. "They'll be coming through here soon." She pulled a paper map from her pocket and unfolded it. A Little dot traveled along the highway right towards them. "We just have to wait."

Lark closed her eyes and let out a relieved sigh. Soon her sister would be back in the city and she could go on about her business. Even if this whole thing started a war for The Order of Fate, Cassie would be out of it. She'll do what her mother wanted her to.

The change in the air caught her attention, and she opened her eyes. Before she could even say anything, her door ripped off the hinges. Cody looked that way and started moving his hand to cast a spell, but before he could, a hand grabbed Lark's arm. The fingers dug into her flesh before it pulled her from the car and into his grasp.

Lark put her hand on his chest and whispered a spell. Fire sprang from her hand and lit the Vampire on fire before he could even react. She turned back to Cody, but he was pushed against the car hood by the same vampire that attacked Cassie only a few days before. She realized who it was holding him down and knew she couldn't help him, so she ran.

Lark pushed back through the outskirts of the city, hoping she could lose and Vampire that might be following. If she could get to Peggy, she might have a chance.

She darted between streets and through alleys. Her lungs burned, but she kept moving until she took a wrong turn into a dead end. She ducked behind a dumpster to try to catch her breath.

Lark closed her eyes and tried to control her breathing, but that same change in the air caught her attention. She opened her eyes and listened, but there was no sound. She shook her head. Something was wrong. The only time there was a change in energy like this, there was a demon not far away. Vampires and demons didn't usually work together.

She leaned forward and peaked around the dumpster, but nothing was there.

"There you are. I've been looking for you. Well, more your sister, but I'll take what I can get," a woman's voice said.

Lark realized she wasn't going to get away so easily and stood. "Who are you?" She could finally see who it was that was haunting her.

The woman stepped out of the shadows, her long blonde hair pulling into a ponytail. She was beautiful, but there was a darkness to her Lark had never seen before.

"I'm the monster your mother warned you about," she said with a smile. "You're the child of the Woman who defied her own kind."

"You leave my mother out of this," Lark hissed.

"Your mother is the key to all of this. If she would have let me kill Cassie when I had the chance her daughter and herself would have lived," the blonde stepped towards her. "You know who I am. Cody told you my story."

"Cody told me your name, and that you were friends," Lark said, not backing down.

"Once." Ami held out her hand. "You can come willingly or... not."

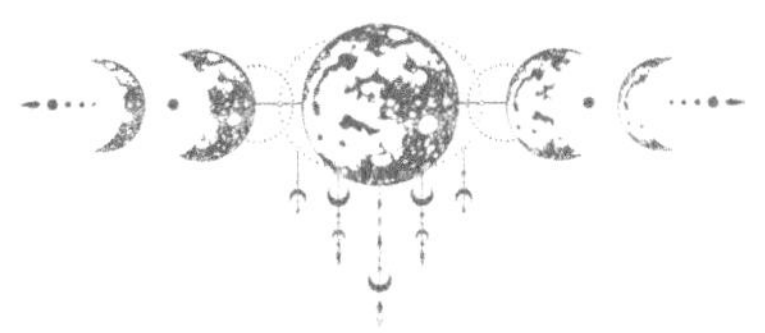

22

Carik

He closed his hands around the steering wheel and stared into the darkness of the night. Cassie would not listen to him and how bad of an idea this was. There were so many that would want her now, and she was walking right into the fire. Why did he even care? She wasn't even one of them. She was a witch and trouble. He sighed as he tried to clear his mind of anything related to Cassie.

"What did you see?" He asked.

She didn't look his way. "My sister is in trouble and I'm the only one that can help her."

"Are you sure?"

She snapped her head in his direction. "You think I don't know what's going on with my sister?"

"It's not that. What makes you think you are the only one that can help her? You have friends, yes?"

"We do, but if I go to them, then I might stop her death

before it happens," Cassie said. "I have to look out for her. She's all I have left."

Carik still had his reservations, but he let them go. If she was doing this, he was doing it with her. They were connected now, and he knew all about how strong Ami really was and what she'd done to his people.

"Do you know anything about Ami?" He asked.

"Nope. No one tells me anything." Cassie sighed and fiddled with something in her pocket.

Carik admired her innocence, but that wasn't what they needed right now. She needed to know what she was up against and what she was getting into.

"Ami was a hunter like you with The Order of Fate. It's part of the reason they call it that. It seems to put people where they are supposed to be." He glanced at her. "Anyway, a demon found her and took an interest in her. He seduced her into becoming like him. The problem was, he wasn't just a vampire. He was the first demon created."

"Yawn, demons are all the same and they die the same with a little magick or a sharp, pointy weapon," Cassie said.

"That's where you're wrong. The first demon can't be killed, only the essence transferred to the next in line," Carik explained. "We learn about it when we're young so we can steer clear of her."

"Are you sure she's even real?" Cassie said. "Of all the Demons I've encountered, I've never heard of her."

"That's because Cody didn't want to tell you about her," a voice said from the back seat.

Carik almost veered into oncoming traffic. "What the fuck?"

"Sorry, you guys were in one place, then another. I couldn't keep up, so I just did this," he said.

"How?" Cassie said, squinting her eyes.

"I'm a demon, duh," he said. "I'm Pycot, by the way."

"Great, good for you." Cassie spun back around. "You know, I could just cast a spell and send you flying out of the car."

"And yet you don't," he teased.

"Why would Cody not tell me about Ami?" Cassie shook her head. "It makes little sense."

"He was protecting her."

"What?" Cassie said. Shocked.

"Maybe more Wesley than her," he said. "They all knew each other. Cody wouldn't want people to know that."

"I don't understand," Cassie said without thinking.

"You're going into battle with the first demon and you don't even know how to kill her, do you?"

Cassie flipped around and stared at him. He gave her a smile and crossed his arms.

"Do you?"

"Do I what?" Pycot shot back.

"Know how to kill her?"

Pycot laughed. "Your boyfriend's right. There's no killing her. You should have run."

"He's not my boyfriend," Cassie snapped.

Carik grumbled without thinking.

"Does he know that?" Pycot said with a smirk.

"Enough of the games, Demon. What are you doing here?" Carik pushed the gas a little harder as he spoke. He would not allow that demon in the car for longer than he had to.

"I wanted to see how this plays out," Pycot answered simply.

"They'll kill you for this," Carik said.

"They already want to for... other things." He didn't elaborate and Carik didn't push him.

"So, you just came to watch?" Cassie shook her head. "No, demons don't think of anyone but themselves."

"If you say so," Pycot said simply.

They sat in silence for the rest of the ride. Cassie noticed the buildings getting larger and the city closing in around them. The first stop was Peggys' place. She'd have everything Cassie needed to take on a demon, first or not.

She stood on the sidewalk in front of the shop, taking it in before turning to the Demon. "You'll have to wait outside," Cassie said.

"Or just leave," Carik finished.

Pycot laughed and shrugged. "I don't want trouble with Peg."

"You know her?" Cassie asked.

"All Demons know of her. She was pretty powerful back in the day," Pycot said before sitting on the curb.

Cassie rolled her eyes and opened the door to the shop. Carik turned back towards the Demon. "You shouldn't be here. I don't want to worry about what you're going to do to Cassie when my back's turned."

"Is that all you're worried about?" Pycot said with a sly smile.

Carik closed the door behind him and leaving the Demon on the street. If he was still there when they were done at Peggys, he would not walk away. One less demon in the world was better for everyone.

23

Cassie

The minute they got in the shop, it felt off. Cassie stopped in her tracks and glanced at the door. "Something's off," she said.

"I've got the door. Yell if you need help," he said, watching her. There was something different in his eyes she hadn't noticed before. It was almost like he cared about what happened to her. She pushed the idea away. Now wasn't the time for that. She needed to find Peggy and whatever was causing the strange energy that filled the shop.

She pushed past a couple of the tables and through the curtain towards the back. To her left was the bed she'd rested on recently. Whatever was happening was happening upstairs in Peggy's private apartment.

It had been a long time since Cassie had gone up there. Long before her mother died, at least. She took a breath as she made her way up the old wood stairs. They creaked with every step, but she kept moving. Once she was at the top, she could see the door leading into Peggy's apartment. It was wide open and there were at least five men in the living room area talking. She tried to sense what they were, but didn't have any luck. Before she could do anything, one turned and looked her way. He was older, probably in his late forties. His dark hair has bits of grey running though it and his light eyes caught her off guard. There was nothing dangerous behind them, only peace she'd never felt before. It was calming, and she yearned for that.

Cassie took a step towards the man. She was so close. So close to peace and freedom, and then Peggy grabbed her shoulders and stepped in front of her.

"Cassie, look at me," Peggy said, shaking her slightly.

Cassie finally broke her gaze and realized she was standing there with Peggy and this group of strangers, all watching her like she was a fish in an aquarium.

"You're okay?" Cassie finally said.

"Yes, I'm fine. You don't look so good, though." She turned and glanced at the man who was staring at me. "You could have killed her."

"She was looking at me. I didn't know she was one of yours," he said before smiling. "You really should tell us these things."

"Why would I tell you anything?" Peggy said, before turning back to me.

"Who are these guys?" Cassie said, rubbing her face. She still was groggy and didn't know what was happening. All she knew was things felt off.

"They're Reapers."

Cassie immediately perked up. "Does that mean someone here is gonna die?" They didn't answer. She looked back at Peggy. "Is Lark here?"

"No, sweetie. I haven't seen her since you left." She glanced at the floor.

"You know something."

"No, I only know what I've been told," Peggy said.

"Witches have died tonight. We were just doing our part by letting Peggy know. She keeps track of that for some reason," the dark-haired Reaper said.

"Who was it?" Cassie demanded.

"I can't tell you that."

"Gareld, she doesn't know the rules," Peggy said.

"Until ten minutes ago, I didn't know there were Reapers," Cassie said.

"The rules of death state we can't tell those that aren't dead the names of the dead. We can only tell them the number and when," Gareld said, annoyed.

"Can you tell me when?" Cassie asked.

"An hour ago at the edge of town."

"That means we just missed it," Cassie said as she started for the door. Peggy grabbed her arm and stopped her.

"You can't stop what's fated," Peggy said.

"You keep saying that, but I can see things too. This isn't how it's going to end for her. I'll make sure of it," Cassie said, shaking off Peggy and running down the stairs and through the shop.

Peggy followed closely behind her." If you are determined to do this, then you will need a few things."

Cassie stopped and really looked at her. Her face was filled with sadness. "I know. That's what I came here for."

Peggy reached behind the counter and pulled out a few potions, and set a box on the table. Cassie knew what it was immediately.

"That's the box. The one they want," Cassie said.

Peggy nodded. "I know. I've hidden it here for a long time."

"Then it needs to stay here. Then Lark won't have it and the Demon won't come for her," Cassie said. She was more hopeful now that she saw the box. It meant what she'd seen hadn't happened yet.

Peggy said nothing. She just smiled slightly. "Here, take these. You'll have a shot to at least get to your sister with them."

Cassie took the potions and nodded. "Thank you."

Peggy grabbed her hand. "I have faith that you will master this new power and save us all."

The statement was chilling. Peggy had never acknowledged there might be a way to change what she'd seen. She always said it was fate, but something was different. Something not even she understood.

"What happened?" Carik said as Cassie flew past him.

"We have to go now," Cassie yelled behind her. "I need to make sure my sister is safe. Cassie debated on whether she should tell Carik about the box. Even without her having it and the gem inside, she was still in danger. They had to find her and get her to safety, then she could figure out what the hell that box was. She stopped short of the car and glanced at Pycot and started pacing.

"What's your issue?" Pycot said, not standing.

"You tracked me. Can you track my sister?"

Pycot stood and shrugged. "Probably. I just need something that is hers."

"What about a sister she'd taken care of her whole life?"

"Using people is tricky. The darkness has to flow through the object or person. It could tear you apart," he said.

"Do it."

Pycot glanced at Carik. "Are you going to let her do this?"

He shook his head. "No, there has to be another way."

"There's not. And I'm not living without my sister. She could be in real danger right now," Cassie said before turning back to the Demon. "Do it."

"We can't do it here. Too many eyes." He sighed. "I know a place, but he will not like it," he said, pointing at Carik.

"I go where she goes." He crossed his arms and waited for the Demon to say something else.

Cassie shook her head. "I don't know what this is, but it has to stop right now. We have a job to do and nothing is going to impede that."

24

Cody

Cody walked over, a bright even though he did not know where he was heading. There was a light in the distance and he headed for that. It was bright, but also warm. A stark contrast to what he was feeling where he was. As he got closer, the surrounding air vibrated with the strongest energy he'd ever felt. He stopped for a moment, but something urged him to keep going. He hesitated and took a step.

A hand grabbed his arm and startled him. He thought he was the only one here. His gaze slid to the dark fingers wrapped around his arm, a dark smoke radiated from them.

"Someone is calling for you," a voice said. He tried to follow the hand to a body with his eyes, but there was only darkness. "But first something that might make your death worth something." The darkness whispered in his ear and he shook his head.

"How do you know I'm looking for that?"

The voice ignored the question. "If you find it, use it. Free the darkness."

"Who are you?" Cody asked.

"A Servent of Death," the scratchy voice stated.

Before Cody could ask questions a green magick wrapped around his body, starting at the feet and working its way up. He felt his body stiffen and the pain surging through him. It was the worst thing he'd ever felt. He closed his eyes and gritted his teeth as it overtook him.

Finally, the pain slowed until all that was left was a massive headache. He felt air fill his lungs as he took a breath in. The cold air on his skin made him flinch.

Cody opened his eyes and was staring at the stars above him. The sound of traffic all around him was jarring.

"That was close," a familiar voice said to his left.

He slowly turned his head, realizing he was laying in the middle of an alley. A familiar face looked back at him, her dark hair pulled into a ponytail and her trademark leather jacket over her black tube top.

Izzy.

"What happened?" Cody managed. He tried to sit up, but the pounding headache put him back down in seconds.

"You died. Vampire, it looked like. You're lucky one of my contacts saw you," Izzy said.

"Contacts?"

She laughed. "We've been friends for a long time. You know I don't always play nice with the Order, but for you, I'd break a few rules."

"You brought me back," he said, finally registering what happened. He forced himself to sit up. "Wesley killed me. He had to of."

"Why didn't you just kill him first?" Izzy said. She was

always very matter of fact with her words. Cody knew friendship meant little to her most of the time. They had a special friendship, though. One that was forged with blood that she wasn't particularly good at talking about.

"I had a truce with them," Cody answered simply.

"That was a long time ago," she sighed. "Looks like the truce is over."

"Looks that way," He said. He put his hand on his head, hoping his magick would help with the pain, but nothing happened. "Why don't I have my magick?"

"It's one of the tricks of death. You just have to wait a bit for it. But the immortal part, that's not something I can fix," she said.

"Did you see anyone else?"

"You mean die?" She asked. She shook her head. "But sometimes the Reapers get there first."

"Damn Reapers," Cody cursed.

Izzy laughed. "Well, technically, I'm the bad guy in that situation." She paused. "When you die, you're supposed to stay dead. I just pull some strings with Death."

"After you've done some favors for him," Cody said.

She smiled. "You do what you have to."

"I've got to go." He stood and everything spun around him.

"You won't get far, not for a while."

Cody sat back down and glanced at Izzy. "How long does this last?"

"A few days, max."

"I can't wait a few days. I have to get back to the Order."

Izzy sighed and shook her head. "You can't even take a break when you're dead," she muttered.

Cody gave her a hard look. "Look, if Wes tried to kill me,

then we're at war and someone has to let The Order of Fate know. They could be attacking them right now."

She rolled her eyes.

"That includes your little friend, Sanora," Cody said.

She snapped her gaze back to him and sighed. "I'll give you a ride."

25

Cassie

Pycot was less than enthused to be taking her wherever he was taking her, but she didn't care. This was the only way they were going to find her sister without alerting Cody she was back. They could have gone back to The Order of Fate, but chances were high Cody was there and he was going to make sure she didn't leave even if Lark was in danger.

Pycot stopped across the street from a club and glanced back at Cassie. "Are you sure you really want to do this?"

Cassie took in the odd-looking club. It looked normal on the outside with a huge neon sign that read Club Vamp. The bouncer standing outside was definitely not someone she wanted to get on the bad side of.

"This is a Vampire club," Carik said.

"Yep." Pycot raised his eyebrows at Cassie. "There are things you might not want to know and if you go in there, there's no turning back."

"What the hell does that mean?" Cassie questioned, but

Pycot didn't answer. She glanced back at the club and nodded. "I have to find Lark."

"Okay, then. Follow my lead."

Cassie followed as Pycot walked across the street, with Carik behind them both. She felt his presence as they got closer. It was something she hadn't realized before. They had some kind of connection and it was growing every minute.

They stopped in front of the bouncer, who looked Cassie up and down. "No Witches allowed. You know the rules."

"She's special. She's Kathrine's Daughter," Pycot cocked his head, and the bouncer looked at Cassie again before looking back at Pycot.

"The little one?" He asked, and Pycot nodded.

The bouncer reached down and pulled the rope up, motioning for them to go inside. Cassie took one more look at him before glancing back to Carik, who shrugged as he followed her inside.

"What was that about?" Cassie asked Pycot.

He didn't stop walking as he spoke. "I told you."

"You didn't tell me anything," Cassie said.

Pycot ignored her and opened the main door to the club. The music immediately made it hard to hear anything else, but the energy was overwhelming and intoxicating. Cassie was almost overtaken by it. The lights flashed with the music. On either side was a pole with a dancer casting light magick with their hands. She wanted to be in the center of it and feel it under her skin. Before she could walk onto the dance floor, Pycot grabbed her and pulled her to the other side of the club. He opened a door and pulled her through to a more private room. Cassie tried to protest, but Pycot gave her a look.

"It's the magick. It's designed to make you want to stay

until the night ends," he said simply. "Give it a minute and it will wear off."

Cassie made a face. For the first time since this had all started, she'd felt free to do what she wanted. What did she want? The fog cleared, and she remembered why they had come there.

"Wait, why did it only affect me?" Cassie asked, looking between Pycot and Carik. They glanced at each other and smiled.

"This is a club for women. Male dancers," Pycot said with a smirk. "I guess we know which way you lean."

Cassie gave him a dirty look. "This is the safe place?"

"Yeah, no one will think anything of a demon raising the energy we need here. And this room is private."

Pycot motioned for Cerik to lock the door. "You can lie down on the couch."

"Do I want to do that?" Cassie asked, making a face. She knew what kinds of things happened in these private rooms. Nothing good.

Pycot held back a slight laugh. "This is my private room here."

"That's supposed to make it better?" Cassie said, without moving.

"It's clean, if that's what you're worried about."

Cassie reluctantly sat on the couch and watched him. He was an interesting demon. Not someone she wanted to get to know, necessarily, but for some reason, she trusted him at least enough to help find her sister.

"You will want to get as comfortable as possible. It's going to hurt, a lot," Pycot said, motioning for her to lie down.

"Fine," she snapped.

Carik stepped closer to Cassie and slid his gaze to Pycot. "If anything happens to her, I'll kill you."

He smiled. "I know."

Pycot took a deep breath.

Then the pain started. It seared straight through Cassie. It was more than she'd ever felt before, even in all her time fighting demons with her mother. It tore through her, splitting her from the place she was. Her mind shot backward in time and she was standing in her childhood home. Her father was writing a letter at his desk. She remembered this. It was before she knew she was a witch. He always spent time at his desk, deep in his work. Cassie never understood what he did. Even after he'd left, they didn't tell her.

She walked around him to see what he was writing. His face was contorted in anger and sadness, but she couldn't make out why or when this was. All she knew was she was happy to see him. She watched his hand as he wrote and couldn't help but read some of the letter.

It was addressed to her mother, and she was confused for a moment.

Why would he be writing her a letter?

This had to be before she was born, when they were dating, maybe. She continued reading it. He talked about how he still loved her and that he would make it work. It didn't matter what she'd done. He still loved her.

"What did she do?" Cassie asked, knowing he couldn't hear her. She reached for the letter, but couldn't grab it. The horrible pain tore through her again and she knew she was being pulled back to herself. She tried to fight it. She wanted to know more, but the more she fought, the harder the present pulled her. She felt herself slam back into her body and yelled out.

Pycot was pulling his energy back, and Carik was rushing Pycot. He shoved him hard and Pycot slammed against the wall. Before anyone could say anything, Carik was holding Cassie in his arms, checking her for any permanent damage. Cassie didn't fight him. She sank into him. His warm body against hers was comforting and for the first time in a long time, she felt safe.

Pycot pulled himself from the floor and rubbed his arm. "If you're interested, I found your sister."

Cassie leaned forward and Carik let her free from his hold. She met Pycot's gaze.

"She's not anywhere I'd want to go, but you being you will probably walk right in," he said.

"Where is she, Pycot," Cassie said.

"She's with the first demon."

26

Lark

She watched Ami from her seat at the far side of the room. She was talking to the Vampire Cody knew from a long time ago. She remembered him from the night they helped Cassie, but he was more loyal than a typical vampire. There was something there she didn't understand and wasn't sure she wanted to. Lark strained to hear them, but they were too far from her.

Ami seemed to notice her watching them and smiled at her.

"Do you need something, human?"

"Not from you," Lark snapped.

Ami laughed and walked towards her. "I will not hurt you, at least not unless your sister makes me. She's the one in control here." She toyed with a strap on her arm. Ami was dressed much how Lark expected. She was in a long dress with a corset top. I gently wrapped the black ribbons from the back of her arms, making the outfit all that more stunning. Her blonde hair was free and her piercing dark eyes laid fixed on her.

Lark turned away, not wanting to give her any reason to continue this conversation.

"When can we expect her?" Ami asked.

"How would I know? She doesn't even know I'm here," Lark said, still looking away.

"I doubt that. Something tells me she knows exactly where you are," Ami said without looking away.

Lark snapped her gaze to Ami and then to Wesley. "What did you do?"

"Me? Nothing." She smiled and reached for Lark's hair. She ran a finger through it. Lark turned away and Ami laughed, still holding the end of the long strand. "Like I said, no one wants to hurt you. I simply need information, and your sister has it. As long as she's willing to tell me what I want to know, you both can go free."

"I don't believe you," Lark said.

"Yet, you believed Cody, and he wanted the same thing," she continued. "Why should I be any different?"

"Cody wasn't trying to kill her." She slid her gaze to Wesley. "He was."

Ami glanced at Wesley and back to Lark. "Are you sure?" Ami smiled and let the lock of hair she'd been holding fall. "It doesn't matter. Your sister will come for you and I'll get my information. Everyone gets what they want." She spun and looked back at Lark. "Isn't that what we all want? To be free of this future that is looming over our heads? Yours with your sister, mine with Wesley. We all want the same thing."

"You have no idea what I want," Lark snapped.

"Then tell me, little girl. What is it you want?" Ami tilted her head and watched Lark.

"To kill you."

"See, we do want the same thing."

27

Cassie

They stood there waiting at an old abandoned warehouse that looked like it was used in a scene from a horror movie and Cassie shook her head. "This can't be the right place."

Pycot sighed. "It is."

Cassie watched him for a moment. "You've been here, haven't you?"

"I told you I wanted to watch how this all played out," Pycot said with a shrug.

"Then why help us?" Cerik asked.

He looked at Cassie before looking back at the warehouse. "I owed your mother a favor. Now that's repaid." He turned to walk away.

"Wait, that's it? You bring us here and then just leave?" Cassie said, confused.

"Yep, good luck."

Before Cassie could say anything else, he was gone.

"We don't need him. We're better off on our own," Carik stated.

Cassie turned back to the warehouse. "Are you sure about that?" She shook her head. "There is no way we're going to beat them, and they probably already know we're here."

"Probably, but if they wanted to kill us, we'd already be dead," Carik said, raising an eyebrow.

"So, do we just walk right in?"

"Seems like it," Carik said.

They stepped into the little street and walked to the warehouse. There was an old metal door close to the street. As soon as Cassie got near it, she could feel the energy. It was cold and dark, like nothing she'd ever felt before. She hesitated.

"What is it?" Carik asked, concern in his voice.

"It's just…" Cassie took a deep breath and opened the door. "A lot of energy."

Carik nodded and took the lead.

As soon as they were clear of the door, it closed behind them.

Cassie glanced at the closed door. There was no turning back now.

They made their way into the large part of the warehouse, but there was no one in the room.

"They have to be someplace nearby," Carik said.

"No, they're here. I can feel them," Cassie said. "The magick that created her is stronger than anything I've ever felt before." She let herself lean into the magick and feel it, hoping it would tell her where to find Lark. She wanted to get her sister and the hell out of there. Then they could figure out what her vision meant and how to stop it. Her gaze closed in on another door at the edge of the building.

Cassie walked towards it and stopped just in front of it. She let out the breath she'd been holding and opened the door. As soon as the door opened, she saw her sister on the other side of that room. Cassie rushed in towards her sister.

"Not just yet," a voice said from her right.

Cassie stopped and snapped her eyes towards the voice. The blonde woman watched her with a smile on her face. She was dressed in a black dress with her light hair pulled away from her face.

"Ami, I presume," Cassie said as Carik came up beside her.

"You brought a friend, good for you," she said with a smirk.

"I'm taking my sister," Cassie demanded.

Ami stepped towards her. "Sure, but first you're going to do something for me."

"No," Cassie said.

"You know you can't beat me. It's better for everyone if you just do what I want. Then you can go on about your life and I can do what I need to do." Ami was so close to her. The magick was strong and dark. It made her so uncomfortable she wanted to take a step back, but knew she couldn't. Carik pulled her back and stepped in front of her.

"Not happening," he said.

Ami sighed. "I really thought you would understand and just do it, but I guess I'll have to force you." She waved her hand and Wesley came up behind them and grabbed Cassie. Carik grabbed Cassie and pulled her away from him. Wesley responded with a huff and pulled Carik to him.

"I hate wolves," he said with disdain.

"Not a fan of Vampires, either," He said as he broke the hold Wesley had on him.

"Get rid of him," Ami yelled as he grabbed Cassie.

Wesley grabbed Carik and threw him through the door to the warehouse.

Ami's fingers dug into Cassie as she pulled her towards her sister. She threw her on the floor and stood behind Lark. "All I wanted was your help. I will let you both leave with no problems once I knew who it was. Once I knew who I needed to find to get rid of this curse."

"Curse?" Cassie said. She shook her head. "I'm not letting you infect anyone else."

"Infect? You want to see what happens when you turn into a vampire?" She slid her hand down Lark's arm. She leaned down and smelled her hair.

Lark shook her head. "Don't tell her anything. I'll be okay."

Cassie slid her eyes from Ami to Lark. "Stop." Cassie pulled one potion from her pocket as she held up her hand and pulled herself to her feet.

Ami raised her head but didn't move from where she was standing. "Well?"

"Step away from her, and I'll do what you want," Cassie said.

"Finally, some cooperation."

Cassie popped the bottle open behind her back and then tossed it at Ami. The bottle exploded and bits of holy water and iron flew in all directions. Cassie grabbed Lark's hand and pulled her towards the door. They were getting the hell out of there.

28

Cody

Cody was not a fan of Izzy and her bike. It went too fast for him even now that he was used to things moving quickly, but she'd offered and he wasn't going to find a better way to get to back to The Order of Fate on his own.

Izzy pulled up in front of the school, but the lights were all out and it was too quiet. Cody stopped outside and felt the energy of the school. It was darker and the wards he put up so long ago were clearly broken. The smell of sulfur filled the air and Cody shook his head.

"Demons," Izzy said. "Your wards should have been strong enough to stop them."

"They may still be inside," he said, heading for the door. Izzy followed as he made his way through the building. Cody pulled a crystal from his pocket. He was surprised he still had to be honest and said an incantation. The stone lit up and light filled the room. Relief flooded him as he realized his magick had come back faster than he thought.

"What about Sanora? Where is she?" Izzy asked. "I haven't been here in a long time."

"I know," he answered simply.

"You used to live here when you first moved to New York."

Cody stopped and felt his stomach tighten. He didn't want to talk about this.

"I know there is a lot of history for you here," Izzy said. "Maggie was the reason it all changed for you."

"Things have for sure changed," Cody said.

"You changed."

"What does that mean?" Cody asked, trying not to be offended.

She laughed slightly. "You used to be all about protecting life and now you're about protecting you."

He turned on her, and she almost ran into him. "I am about protecting life. I do what I do to keep people alive. Just like I've always done."

She stared at him for a moment. "You realize when I bring a person back from the dead, I can see everything. Everything is good. Everything bad."

Cody held her gaze for a moment before turning back down the hallway, looking silently into each room.

"Look, I get it. I haven't done things the right way my whole life either. Sometimes it comes down to who is more important to the world."

"Maggie was important to the world and look how that ended."

"That was some rogue vampire trying to impress the boss." Izzy said. "I thought you would learn something from that and how you operate." She stopped. "I know you think you did what you had to do with her, but she was a mother."

"That sounds so horrible when you put it that way," he said.

"But you know it's true. It's unfortunate she died, though."

"That wasn't the plan," Cody said without thinking. "It was supposed to be the kid."

"But it wasn't," Izzy said, turning into one of the rooms.

"I know. I've lived with that every day since."

"But you never told Lark or Cassie," Izzy stated. "That's not going to be something you can just ignore."

"How would I even tell them? Yeah, sorry, I'm responsible for your mother's death." He cringed when he finally said it out loud.

"Maybe, but I'm telling you when they find out, it's going to be over for you."

"I'm not living much longer," he muttered. "Wesley will make sure of that. At least I can take him with me when I go." He stopped and turned back around. "There's no one here. They probably went to the safe houses."

"That's a good thing at least," Izzy said. "I'll find Senora. I could give two shits about any of the others here. That's your job."

Cody watched as she walked out of the building. He sighed as he made his way to his office. Everything was still intact. They hadn't been looking for him. He shook his head. Now he was sure it was Ami who sent the Demons here. They thought he was dead. Cody couldn't help but smile. It would be interesting when he showed up to kill them.

Izzy was right. He'd changed, and it wasn't for the better. But now he had the information he needed. The thing that could finally kill the evil he'd spent his whole life protecting the world from. He just had to get it before the one who had it realized what it was.

He pulled out an old book he'd gotten once from one of the original founders of the Order. It was over five hundred years old and bound in the hide of their sacred deer. The seal of the Order of Fate greeted him as he opened the pages.

The story of the first demon was in this book.

* * *

A boy no older than ten raced through the sacred forest, his body painted red and white to honor his transition from boy to man. His bare feet hit the ground, pushing the moss and wood of the forest away. His dark hair was long and loose, with only a single small braid made on the left of his face. This was the symbol of his clan and his status as a new warrior, if he could face the darkness within himself.

He jumped the creek and stopped taking in the world around him. It was quiet except for a few birds in the trees. The sun was going down and he would be alone for the night. That was the custom, the ritual that would make him worthy to be a warrior finally.

He pulled some sticks together and started a fire before the sun completely disappeared. The boy listened and waited for the Darkness as they called it. Some heard it, some didn't, but they all had to face it.

It didn't take long before the voices started.

Isla, we've been waiting for you.

"I'm not falling for your tricks," the boy said, watching the water. It was dark, but the sounds of the rushing water comforted him.

I offer no tricks, only the ability to save everyone.

The boy shook his head. "No, you offer lies."

The laugh that echoed through the forest brought chills to him. I am many things, but I'm no liar.

Isla kept his eyes on where the water was trying to tune the voice out. The water kept him calm. He breathed slowly, waiting for his trial to end, but the water slowly lit up with a beautiful blue light. He walked to the edge and peered into it.

A turquoise stone glowed at the bottom, and he smiled. It was amazing.

take it.

He shook his head. "I can't take it,"

Why? Because someone told you not to?

He stared at it and bit his lip. The stone seemed to call to him, to want to give him its magick. He stepped into the water and dove into it.

It's yours if you want it. All of it. The power to save everyone you love. Take it.

He reached out for it, but hesitated.

You are chosen. Take it.

He let his fingers slid over the stone before pulling it from the water. The power of it surged through him and he gasped. Then there was nothing but pain.

29

———

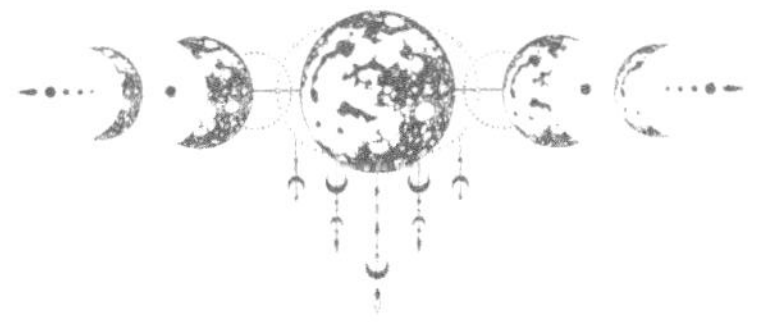

Carik

He hit the ground hard, but didn't think too much. Carik knew the Vampire would be right on him. He rolled to the side and jumped up as Wesley came at him. The Vampire swung at Carik and he dodged it.

"Is that the best you got, vampire?" He teased. "I thought you were the one to watch out for."

Wesley said nothing, but a smile crossed his face. He ran at Carik, moving faster than any vampire he'd ever seen before. Carik couldn't even react before he felt a punch to his ribs and the unmistakable sound of ribs cracking. He folded and fell to his knees.

"Not so chatty now, are you?" Wesley said, leaning over him. "I expected more of a fight from a wolf, but I guess all the violence was bred out of you."

"You want to see violence?" Carik choked out. He closed his eyes and fell deep into himself. The animal inside him begged to be free, and this time he wasn't going to deny it.

His bones cracked and bent as his body rearranged

itself. He dug his hands into the cement floor to fight the pain. It had been a while since he shifted and the familiar pain pulsed through him. Before he had time to process it, the pain leveled out, and he opened his eyes. Everything was brighter and more defined. The air in his lungs felt cooler and calm. Now he could feel the energy Cassie had been talking about.

Cassie, he had to save her. The wolf demanded it.

He turned towards Wesley, who took a step back. That magick that made Ami what she was visible to him now. He could see it running through his veins. It was in Wesley's blood. All Carik had to do was take a bite and all that strengthened him than other vampires would pour from his veins. He snarled and stepped towards Wesley.

Before Wesley could react, he was on top of him. Carik growled before biting Wesley below the chin, ripping his throat out.

Wesley pushed back and threw Carik against the wall. He stood and put his hand up to survey the damage. "You really think a bite will kill me?" he laughed.

Carik stepped back and watched the magick drain from his body before running at him again. This time, he grabbed at his leg and pulled him to the ground. Wesley fought back, hitting and pushing at the Wolf, but it was no use. Carik bit the side of neck and didn't let go. He shook his head, ripping the flesh apart. Wesley reached up and grabbed at the Wolf's paw, twisting it hard. Carik kept ripping at Wesley's neck until he was completely through and Wesley stopped moving.

Carik stepped back, and the Vampire turned into a pile of dust.

He heard a loud explosion and tilted his head towards

the door. Cassie and Lark ran through it. He locked eyes with Cassie and relief flooded through him. She was alive.

"Carik? We have to go," Cassie yelled at him and he followed them out of the warehouse. He jumped in front of them and ran through the streets, charting a safe path for them. They weren't far from Peggy's, and that was the only place he felt was safe in the entire city for them.

Cassie and Lark ran into the store and Carik made his way through before they were met with Peggy. She hurried past them and locked the door. He watched as she moved the carpet in front of the door and drew a rune on the floor. It turned red before disappearing into the wood. Peggy let the carpet fall back over the spot and glanced at him.

"You're going to need something to wear," she said.

30

Cassie

Cassie pulled her sister into the back of the shop and sat her on the bed. She looked her over and Lark shook her hands and pushed her away.

"I'm fine," Lark said, not looking at Cassie.

"What happened?" Cassie demanded.

Lark glanced up at her and shook her head. "Nothing. She insisted she wanted to just get information and send us away."

Cassie sat beside her. "Did she hurt you?"

Lark shook her head. "But I don't know what happened to Cody. We were waiting for you at the edge of the city. We were going to all see if what she said was true."

"You mean see if they could take the book out of me?" Cassie stared at her for a moment. "You were in on it?"

Lark sighed and shook her head. "I just wanted to keep you safe. I didn't..."

"You underestimated her," Carik said, walking into the back. He was dressed in a dark pair of dress pants and a dark button-down shirt. Cassie smiled and raised an eyebrow.

"Nice outfit," she said with a laugh.

Carik made a face.

"It's something I had," Peggy snapped. "You can stay here for a while, but you'll have to get out of the city before long. The invisibility spell won't last forever."

"We'll stay for the night and figure it out in the morning," Carik said. "I'll keep watch. You two should get some sleep."

Cassie glanced at Lark, who normally knew what to do, and nodded. She'd never seen Lark like this. Usually, it was her taking care of Cassie and keeping her safe. She'd never seen Lark so fragile, not even after their mom had died.

Cassie glanced at Peggy. "I need a quiet place to see something," she said.

"You can use my apartment. I'll stay with Lark," Peggy said, taking a seat beside Cassie's sister.

Cassie smiled and turned to walk up to Peggy's apartment. She'd only used the magick in the book a few times like this, but she needed to know what to do next. If she could only see into the future just a little, she'd know the next move and how to help her sister and herself.

She closed the door to Peggy's apartment behind her. The room was good sized with the old comfy couch she'd fallen asleep on so many times when she was little. Infront of it was a small table with some books on it. Peggy didn't own a television, so books were how she escaped the world. Cassie smiled as she thought of the time Peggy had accidentally read a spicy romance novel to Lark and her when her mother was gone on one of her trips.

She sat in the center of the room to the left of the little table and took a breath. She thought of right now and let herself fall deep within. She was standing in that blackness again; the book sat open in front of her. Cassie reached out with her hand and let the magick push through her. It was stronger than before. Almost as if they finally were forming a bond. She felt her body fall and opened her eyes.

Cassie was standing outside the shop. The street was empty except for an orange tabby who hissed at her. She cocked her head.

"You can see me?"

The cat growled and stepped back before it cowered under her. Cassie stepped back, feeling a bit sad she'd scared a kitty, but she couldn't help it. The animal knew she wasn't supposed to be there. She took a breath and looked up and down the street. At least she was in the right timeframe.

The door opened to the shop and someone she knew came out. Cassie gasped as she watched her light hair fall into her face and Peggy following right behind.

"Mom?" Cassie said, rushing to her.

Her mother turned on Peggy. "I need to do this. It's important."

"More important than your girls?" Peggy snapped.

"Mom, it's me. It's Cassie," Cassie said desperately as she stood in front of the two women.

"It's because of the girls. I have to know who killed him," her mother said.

"We know who it was. You just can't see it, Kat," Peggy answered. She grabbed her arm. "I've seen where this road leads. You can't do this. It will change everything for your children."

"I know what I'm doing," Kat snapped as she pulled her arm away. "You're wrong. Sanir would never do something like this. He loves me."

"Sanir is a Warlock. He doesn't love. You know that whole marriage was a sham and the fact he admitted to you, he knew." Peggy shook her head. "You know it was him."

"Sanir loved his daughter. He'd never do anything to hurt her," Peggy said.

"And what about Cassie? Would he hurt her?" Peggy spat.

Kat's face contorted and tears threatened to fall down her face. "I loved him, Peggy. It was the realist thing I've ever felt. I can't just walk away."

"Wayo would understand. He'd want you to protect her." Peggy softened and pulled Kat into her arms.

"Cassie can't know," Kat whispered into Peggy's shoulder.

Cassie stepped backwords shaking her head. She felt sick, like someone had just ripped away everything she'd known. Who was Wayo and why didn't anyone tell her about him? What was going on? She glanced back at her mother and Peggy. She was pulling her back into the shop. Once the door closed, Cassie collapsed on the road and felt herself falling. She closed her eyes and shook her head.

"It's not true. My mom wouldn't lie to me."

"But she did," Peggy's voice said from beside her.

Cassie opened her eyes and slid her gaze to Peggy. She was sitting on the floor beside her. "You knew, and you didn't say anything."

"Your mother didn't want anyone to know. She wanted the world to think you were Sanir's daughter," Peggy said.

"Why?"

"Because he has influence and that would protect you."

"But he left too," she whispered. "I never realized he wasn't my father."

"That was a spell."

"What?" Cassie felt like everything she'd ever been told was a lie. "You knew I was going to find out. You knew I'd see it."

Peggy nodded. "I hoped your mother would eventually tell you."

"Who was he?"

Peggy smiled. "I never met him. Your mother went to a coven meeting the Witches in Atlanta were holding. She wasn't a part of The Order of Fate back then. She was on her way to become the next leader of the Coven here in New York." Peggy smiled. "She met Wayo there, and they fell for each other."

"Why did I see it? Why now?" Cassie felt like her entire world had already changed and he she was dealing with another thing to add to it.

"I don't know, but I knew you would be there at that moment. I just didn't realize how."

"You didn't know about the book?"

"Not then. After that moment happened, and I saw you in my own visions, I looked for how. I ran across some talks about a witch who could travel to the future and the past. I'm not sure how it works. There wasn't any information on that." Peggy smiled. "The wolfs are very secretive about their lore."

"That's the other thing I don't understand. Why are the Wolves so involved?"

Peggy shrugged. "I'm not sure, but I think it dates back to when they were working with witches. Maybe it's something left from the truce."

Cassie sighed. She was so overwhelmed with everything and still had to keep herself alive. She had to know what the next move would be, but if she went back into the future, she was worried it would just tell her more things she didn't want to know.

"I know that look," Peggy said. "I get it every time I have to go into the future."

"I know you can't say anything, but I have to know what the next move is," Cassie said.

"I know." Peggy smiled. "You know it's not that I can't say anything, but if I do, then you may not make the choices you need to make. Having that knowledge is difficult. Make hard choices and sometimes they can get people killed."

Cassie watched the old woman for a moment. She felt like that was a loaded statement, but brushed it off.

"I'll let you get back to it, but just know that whatever you see, you make the choices."

31

Pycot

He sat at the bar with a drink in his hand. The bar tender wasn't anywhere to be seen, but that was typical in a place like this. This bar was one of those that you didn't tell people you came to.

Pycot took a drink and messed with the napkin on the bar in front of him. He'd just left them to figure it out. Never had he feared any demon or anything, but feeling that energy, he wasn't about to jump into the den of the First Demon and die. Not for anyone.

But still, that feeling of guilt picked at him. He'd seen so much in his lifetime. The building of this city being a highlight, but one person had made him think of all the crap he was doing and why. Demons didn't think about that much. They just did what they do, but Kat had been something different. When she paid him to take her to the underground of the Demon world, he knew she was something special. Too bad she didn't feel that way about him.

He smiled at the thought of her, but the smile faded

when he thought about what she'd think of him just leaving her daughters to face Ami on their own.

She would hate him for it.

Pycot sighed and pushed the drink away. He had a card to play with Ami, and maybe he could use it to find out exactly what the fuss was about with this person she was looking for.

If she didn't kill him first.

32

Cassie

She watched Peggy leave and settled back into the blackness where the book still lived in her mind. It was open in front of her and she put her hand on it. The magick infused with her and the book fully disappeared. She felt the heat of the energy course through her before she closed her eyes.

When she opened them, she could see everything. Timelines raced before her eyes. They moved so fast she could barely make them out. First, a man with his children in a park, the Eiffel Tower behind him. Then a woman crying in front of the ocean.

She took a deep breath, pulling the energy and forcing the images to slow. It settled on the little shop. She could see Lark laying in the small bed downstairs and Carik keeping watch through the store windows. Peggy was looking through the things behind the counter. She picked up that box with the weird stone Cassie had seen Lark with when she died and put it to the side. Even when she was like this, the box pulsed with power. Whatever was in there was something she would not be able to ignore forever.

She concentrated and felt time slip forward just a little, but somehow there was a gap between what was and what was going to be. Cassie tried again to see, and it skipped it again.

It annoyed Cassie. She couldn't get a straight answer and pushed the power hard. She felt a blinding pain in her head, forcing her to close her eyes. When she opened them, she was standing in the shop, but it was all wrong. The door was gone, and they shattered the glass in the windows on the floor. She was back in that horrible future she'd seen too many times.

Cassie sighed and walked out of the shop. Everything was quiet, and the city was destroyed. She walked towards The Order of Fate. If anything, that would still be standing. Knowing Cody, he'd have it all set up to defend the Witches of New York at the very least. Maybe she could get a sense of when this was going to happen.

She walked through the streets, watching every corner for life, but there was nothing. No people, no cars, nothing. As Cassie got further into the city, she noticed the buildings looking better, more lived in, but still no one she could see. The sun beat down on her and she felt like she was going to get sick. *I guess I get the full experience.*

Finally, the Order was within sight. She hurried to it, but something was wrong. The magick that once surrounded it was gone and all the windows had some kind of a metal curtain over them, keeping the sun out. She shook her head.

"This is all wrong."

Cassie made her way to the door, and to her surprise, it opened. She walked in and looked around her. Everything looked normal on the inside. It was clearly being used. Maybe the new leader of the Order of Fate had put in these security measures. Maybe humans were in control of it again.

She rounded the corner and stopped in the hallway where the rooms were. What if she didn't want to see what was behind these doors? Cassie shook off the thought and put her hand on the doorknob. She slowly opened the door and walked inside.

A woman in a white jumpsuit was lying on the bed. To the right of the door. There was nothing else there but her and a bed. Cassie thought that was strange, but when she took a step closer, something else came over her. This girl wasn't a witch, but she wasn't a demon, either. She was something else.

"I don't know what kind of game you're playing, but I know you're there," she said, not moving.

"You can see me?" Cassie said without thinking.

"No, but I can feel you." The woman sat up. "What are you?"

"It's complicated," Cassie answered. "You're not a Witch?"

"No, no one's seen a witch in thirty years."

"What are you?" Cassie said, without missing a beat.

"It's complicated," she smarted off. "I'm the thing that can kill all vampires."

"All?"

The girl nodded, looking all over the room. "All."

"What's your name?" Cassie asked, watching her.

"Grace," she answered. "My mom saved me."

Cassie smiled. "Mine too." She felt herself being pulled and tried to fight it. "Who are you fighting?"

"Fighting? Vampires," Grace answered.

The pull got stronger. "No, the leader. What's their name?" She pushed back against the pull and felt herself slide back to Grace.

"I don't know his name. I'm sorry."

"My name is Cassie. Find me if I'm still alive." Cassie felt the pull yank her hard, and she fell backwards. Her chest heaved with pain. It was like she'd been hit with a baseball bat. She struggled to catch her breath and laid on the floor for what seemed like forever.

Then she heard the window break.

33

Ami

She pulled the shards of iron from her skin and threw them on the ground. That bitch had actually used iron on her. She rolled her eyes. Wrong demon for that.

She felt a stabbing in her heart and grabbed her chest. She knew exactly what it was. They hurt Wesley. He needed her. She'd get those girls later. It's not like they could outrun her.

She rounded the corner and raced through the door. When she saw the pile of ash on the ground, she felt her heart shatter. Everything that made her human was gone, and she was alone. Ami fell to her knees and ran her fingers through the ash. She felt tears well up in her eyes, but fought them back.

She would not let them just give her the information she wanted and leave; she was going to destroy them.

"What happened?" Pycot said from the other side of the warehouse. He hurried towards her as she glanced at him.

"They killed him. Wes is gone," Ami managed. She stood and wiped her face. "Now they're going to die."

Pycot took a step back and looked from the ash to Ami. "What are you going to do?"

"I'm going to get the information I need. Even if it means everyone in this city dies," Ami said, looking at him. "But that's not what you want to hear, is it?"

"What do you mean?" Pycot said, taking a step back.

"You think I come to a city and don't know everything about it?" She smiled and slowly walked towards him. He stepped back as she advanced. "You're thing with Kat was very well known, especially with the people I work with."

"That was a long time ago," Pycot answered.

"Not long enough," a voice said from behind him.

Ami smiled and crossed her arms. "You know all about Sanir, I'm sure."

Pycot turned, looked at him and then back to Ami before dissolving into water and slinking away. Sanir turned and raised his arm to do a spell before Ami stopped him.

"Let him go. There's nothing he can do now." She turned to Sanir and smiled. "We can both have what we want."

"I'm sorry about Wesley," Sanir Said and Ami faltered slightly.

"I know who killed him and this time, they won't be able to get away."

34

Cassie

She raced down the stairs and into the back of the shop. By the time she got there, she could see the commotion of the fight. She couldn't see what was happening, only that Carik, Lark, and Peggy were on one side and the attacker on the other.

Cassie pushed through the hallway and ran into the shop. She turned her head to the attacker behind the counter in confusion.

"Cody?" Cassie shook her head as he put his hand up and an energy vibration came at her. She couldn't see it, but she could feel it. The force of it knocked her down.

"I'm sorry. I need this," he said as he pulled the box with the gem inside from behind the counter.

"You have no idea what you're doing," Peggy said, still standing by the entrance to the back of the shop.

"If you are as powerful of an Oracle as they say, you know I can't just sit back and watch," Cody snapped. I have to do something. I was there when Ami was created and I'm going to be there when she'd undone."

"That's not how things work," Peggy snapped.

Cody didn't say anything. He just grabbed one of Peggy's potions and threw it at the wall behind them. The air filled with smoke and Cassie coughed.

Before she could even open her eyes, Carik was there, holding on to each side of her.

"Are you okay?" His voice was soothing and calm.

Cassie smiled. "I'm fine, but we have to get that box back."

Carik shook his head. "It's not important. We have to get out of the city."

"You don't understand. That box is what Lark gets killed for," Cassie said. "A Demon kills her for it."

"All the more reason for all of us to get out of here before it's too late," Carik answered. "If Lark and you aren't here, then no one dies."

"If only it were that easy," Peggy said.

Cassie snapped her eyes up to her. She was staring towards the door of the shop. Cassie followed her gaze to someone she recognized. His energy was darker now, full of hate and malice, and it seemed to be directed straight at her.

"Dad?" Lark said, not moving.

He looked at her and smiled. "My daughter. I've missed you." He looked back at Cassie and he sighed. "You have caused enough trouble." He raised his hand and Cassie was pulled to him. He grabbed her arm and pulled her to her feet.

Carik was on his feet and reaching for Cassie before anyone else could react except for Sanir. All he had to do was put his hand in front of Cassie and all the air was pulled from her lungs. She grasped and fought to breathe, but couldn't.

"You're all invited, but if anyone does something stupid, Cassie won't be alive long," He said and Carik stepped back. Sanir released the magick and Cassie gasped for air. He looked at Lark and sighed. "I hope you can understand my position with Cassie."

She looked at him, disgusted. "Cassie's my sister."

"And I'm your father." He looked at Peggy. "I suppose you know what happens next."

She smiled. "I do, and you will be very disappointed."

Sanir smiled. "I doubt that." He whispered something, and Peggy's eyes rolled back. She grabbed at the air before falling to the ground.

"This might be jarring," he said before whispering something under his breath.

The shop blurred, and the air got hot. So hot that Cassie was afraid to breathe. Her skin felt like it was burning from her body until she felt the air cool and the familiar room came into focus. Standing in front of them was Ami.

She smiled and cocked her head. "Now, I'm going to get what I want and you're all going to die."

Sanir threw Cassie forward, and she fell on her knees in front of Ami. "As you saw already, Sanir is a powerful warlock. So, now it doesn't matter if you tell me what I want to know. He'll make you." Ami sighed and looked at Carik. "You. You killed Wesley." She sauntered towards him. "Now you're going to scream. I hate wolves, but you just won't die out."

"We're survivors," Carik said, not breaking her gaze. Ami just smiled and looked at Sanir. "Make him scream."

He smiled and held his hand up. He twisted it and Carik fell forward, his face contorting in pain. He held it in the best he could, but Cassie could see it on his face. He wasn't going to give Ami the satisfaction of a scream.

Ami bent down to him and made a pouty face. "Why aren't you screaming? It would all stop if you did."

"Stop," Cassie yelled. She couldn't take it anymore. "Just stop hurting him."

Ami snapped her gaze to Cassie and then back to Sanir. He dropped his hand and turned back to Cassie. "Is it your turn already?" Ami stood in front of her before grabbing her hair and pulling her to her feet. "Tell me who I need to transfer this curse to."

It wasn't what she expected to hear. "What?"

Ami pulled her hair tighter and Cassie squirmed. "Tell me what I need to give this curse to."

Cassie nodded, "Okay."

Ami let go of her hair and watched her.

Cassie glanced at Sanir and then back at her. "I can't do it with everyone here."

"Remember when I said you didn't have to..." Ami smiled and then all Cassie felt was pain. She fell to the ground as the pain pushed through her. Her head felt like it was splitting in half. She tried to fight against it, but it made it worse. She felt herself falling and then she was lying on the ground.

"Get up," Sanir said.

Cassie opened her eyes and realized they weren't in the warehouse anymore, but they didn't look like they were in the future either. "Where are we?"

"We are still in the warehouse, but you are where the next one is," Sanir snarled at her.

"The one Ami wants to give her a curse too," Cassie said, without thinking. She stood and followed Sanir's gaze to a playground. A young boy maybe eight years old was swinging alone. "I'm not letting her give that curse to a child."

Sanir didn't look at her. "Some children are a curse. They have no true purpose except to destroy families."

"You're talking about me now," Cassie said, shaking her head.

"Your mother was... suitable. Our children would be strong with magick." He looked at her and curled his lip in disgust. "Then she had to have that fling with that thing."

"Thing?" Cassie had never felt this much hate from him. When she was little, he'd been warm and giving. At least that was what she thought.

"I should have taken Lark and left you and your mother to rot."

"Why didn't you?" Cassie kept her eyes on the boy.

He didn't answer the question and Cassie felt the pain in her head again. She fell to the ground and was back kneeling in front of Ami.

"Well?" she said.

"It's a child. A boy. I can take you to him," Sanir said, before Cassie could even think.

"You can't do this to a child," Cassie finally said.

Ami glanced down at her. "I don't care who they are. It's time for me to be done with this."

"You'd really give it to someone that can't even live on their own yet?" Cody said as he walked into the warehouse. He was holding the box he'd stolen from Peggy's.

Ami's eyes went to it and back to Cody. "You really think that will kill me?"

Cassie shifted her gaze to him and then looked back to Lark standing behind Carik. He had pulled himself up to his knees and was watching her. She looked back at the scene in front of her and tried to stand. Sanir pushed her back down.

"I don't know," Cody said.

"You're willing to die to find out?" Ami said, taking a step towards him.

Cody held his ground. He glanced at Cassie and then Lark. Cassie knew that meant he was about to do something he'd regret.

Cody dropped the box on the ground and lunged at Ami. He's been holding the stone the whole time and reached for her chest. She pushed him down and the stone rolled towards Cassie.

Ami grabbed Cody's shoulders and pulled him to her before sinking her fangs into his neck.

Cassie grabbed the stone and threw it towards Carik. He grabbed and stared at Cassie. She shook her head, and he handed it to Lark. Sanir grabbed Cassie's arm and yanked her towards him. Lark hesitated.

"I wouldn't," Sanir said. "Give it to me."

Ami dropped Cody's body and kept her eyes on Cassie.

Lark shook her head. "No."

He yanked Cassie hard.

"You're going to kill her anyway," Lark said. "At least I can stop her." Lark looked at Cassie and nodded.

"No, no. Don't do this Lark," Cassie said.

"You know I have to," Lark answered before she cast a spell and bright light filled the room. When Cassie could open her eyes, Lark was gone. Cassie didn't know if this would be the last time she'd seen her sister. She didn't know if this was the moment she died, but there was no other choice. Lark didn't give her one.

Sanir threw Cassie on the ground.

"Wait, before you kill her, I want her to see what her information brings. I want her to see it all."

35

Lark

She ran from the warehouse, tears streaming down her face. She'd just left her sister to die by her father's hand. How could she wrap her head around that? She didn't even know where she could go. Peggy's was the only place she could think of, but it would be the first place they would look for her. She stopped a few blocks from the warehouse to catch her breath.

Lark listened and waited, but didn't hear anything. She closed her eyes and the magick from the stone filled her hand. It was like nothing she'd ever felt before. Complete creation not just of evil, but of everything. She put it in her pocket and started running again.

Lark swung around the corner and could finally see Peggy's store. The front windows were blown out, and the door was completely gone. As she got closer, she could see movement inside and froze. The smell of sulfur filled the air. Demons.

She stepped backwards and ran into something hard.

When she turned, she saw the ugliest demon she'd ever seen. It was mostly goo formed into a worm shape. Not even the one that had killed her mother looked so horrible. The smell was a mix of sulfur and ash. It made her gag as she stepped away from it.

"It wants the stone," she heard from her left. She glanced that way as she stepped back and could see what looked like a man, but clearly wasn't one when you looked into his eyes. He was tall with dark hair that was slicked back and wearing dark blue jeans. She didn't have time to take him in before something was flying at her.

The man, demon, put his hand out and formed a wall of water between her and the slimy demon. Why was he helping her?

"Get out of here," he yelled, and she ran. She didn't know where she was running to, but she just ran. Everything felt hopeless. She wasn't sure what she should be doing next, and she wasn't sure if she would ever see her sister again. The only thing she knew was now it was up to her to make sure Ami never killed anyone again. Her sister would be the last death from Ami if she had anything to say about it.

She rounded a corner and realized she was at a dead end. She turned, but the slimy demon was standing at the edge. She had no way out. Lark stepped back until she was against the wall. The only thing she had was her magick, but it wasn't particularly strong.

Lark felt around in her pocket. She knew she had a potion she'd swiped from Peggy's. Her fingers curled around the little bottle and she pulled it from her pocket.

The slimy demon was getting closer, so she readied herself for the fight.

The smell of sulfur filled the air, and she covered her

nose. She caught a puddle of water forming something to her right and stepped as far away as she could. When it was done forming, she realized it was the Demon from before.

He put his hands out and shook his head. "I'm here to help you."

"Why?" was all she could manage.

"Long story," he answered.

She raised her eyebrows.

He sighed. "I'm Pycot. I knew your mother." He pointed at the slimy demon. "I'll explain more later. That's a Salitos. Aim for the eye."

"What eye?" All Lark saw was slimy parts.

"Center of the head," Pycot shrugged. "Just the top of it."

Pycot pulled the water from the ground, and it floated in front of them. Lark watched it for a moment in wonder. She'd never seen anyone do that in all the years she'd been near Witches and her mom. It was beautiful until the water droplets came together and formed what looked like a spear. She glanced at Pycot and he looked back at her.

"What?" He said.

Lark looked back at the Demon barring down on them.

"We'll only get one shot at this," Pycot said. "Now." The spear flew forward at the slime Demon and Lark threw the potion. Both impacted it at the same time. The bottle shattered at the point of the spear right before it went through what Lark figured was its eye. The slime boiled and bubbled before falling to the ground in a pile of goo.

"Gross," Lark said before looking at Pycot. He smiled and Lark couldn't help but feel relief. That was until she felt the shooting pain in her chest.

Pycot's face twisted as he registered what was happening. He caught her as she started to fall.

She turned her head to see what had happened, but

another large slime demon was standing there. It sucked the stone into itself before Pycot was on his feet. She smelled the sulfur in the air and watched as the slime demon exploded. She wasn't sure what had happened, but before she could say anything, Pycot was kneeling over her.

"It's not that bad. I know a healer that will fix you right up," he said, trying to pull her up. The pain shot through her and the air was cold.

She shook her head. "I can't... move," she got out. "Cassie."

"No, I'm supposed to keep you safe."

Lark laughed slightly. "I don't even know you."

"No, but I know you and you are not dying," he said, again pulling at her to stand.

She winced from the pain. "Save Cassie. I'll wait here."

Pycot shook his head. "No, that's not how this works."

"Ami... is going to kill her. We don't both need to die today," Lark said. She felt so cold, and it was hard to stay awake. She fought it. She didn't want to leave her sister.

Lark, it's okay, baby.

"Mom?" She looked around her for her mother. She swore she heard her. The cold fingers wrapped around her and her vision faded.

It's okay.

36

______

Cassie

She sat against the wall watching Sanir who would occasionally pace the entire room. Cassie crossed her arms over her knees and pulled them to her. All she could think about was how she'd sent Lark away and what was going on with her. Was she okay?

She glanced at Carik, who was kneeling. Cassie could see the pain he was dealing with but was glad he was still alive. What kind of damage Sanir caused? She didn't know.

"Why did the Warlocks and witches need a truce?" Cassie said, out of nowhere. If she was going to be stuck in this room with her stepfather, she might as well get some kind of knowledge of the past. It's not like any of them told her anything.

He met her gaze and sighed. "You don't know your history?"

"No one tells me anything," she snapped.

"Warlocks were once the most powerful beings in

magick, but women Warlocks started dying out. We were forced to either mate with witches or... humans."

"So you made a truce," Cassie finished on her own.

"It was the only way to rebuild the bloodline," Sanir said.

"Good thing Lark is a witch," Cassie said with a smirk.

He said nothing. "You have no idea how things work. You think you know the world, but all you know is what your coward mother taught you," Sanir seethed.

"What would you know about her?"

"I know she died protecting you," He looked her up and down. "You and your tainted blood."

"Look, I know I'm not your kid, but I never even knew this guy who apparently was my birth father. I only knew you and I loved you for some unknown reason," Cassie snapped.

"The spell I put on you. To keep you from seeing me until I was ready," He said.

"Well, thank you for that, because at least I got some-thing of a father," Cassie muttered.

"I am not your father."

"Clearly," Cassie snapped.

She said nothing else and just stared at him. He had looked so good and loving all those years ago, but it was all a lie. She wasn't sure how she felt about that. It was such a betrayal. She didn't have time to think about it before the door opened and Ami walked in with the boy following behind her. Cassie watched him with fear in her eyes. He was a child and Ami was ready to make him the first demon without caring at all about how he was going to handle it.

"Jared, come and sit. You've had a long day," Ami said without looking at him.

"You can't be serious," Cassie said without thinking, and Sanir shot her a dirty look.

Ami smiled and raised her hand. "I thought about what you said and you're right. I can't turn him as a child, but he won't always be." She smiled. "I'll teach him and then, when he's the right age, release myself from this curse."

Cassie stood and took a step towards Ami. "He's just a child."

"He is, for now, but you don't need to worry about that." Ami took a step towards Cassie and put her hand on her shoulder. "You'll be dead soon." She turned to Sanir and sighed. "A deal is a deal. You can do what you want with them."

Sanir smiled and grabbed Cassie's arm. "Finally, I can get rid of you. Then the Wolf." He pulled her from the room and into the larger part of the warehouse.

Cassie didn't fight it. She felt defeated and done. It didn't matter what she did or wanted to do; she would not change anything. What was the point of this power? All she knew was what was going to happen so many years later. How was that going to help her?

He threw her to the ground, and she just sat there. She glanced at Sanir standing over her when her vision faded a little and the picture of the father she'd known so many years ago was sitting at his desk. He looked at her with something in his eyes and it wasn't the rage she was seeing in him right now. It was with compassion and caring. Cassie smiled. "I'm sorry. I love you."

Her vison snapped back, and she locked eyes with the Sanir from the present. He had his hand up ready to cast the magick that would kill her, but there was hesitation in his dark eyes.

It was just enough time for the water puddle on the floor

to change into the Demon that Cassie trusted, even though he was just that, a demon.

Pycot pushed a wall of water at Sanir, and he slammed into the wall. Pycot then reached his hand out and pulled Cassie to her feet. He held out the stone he had and Cassie's stomach fell.

"Lark?" she asked, even though she knew the answer.

He didn't say anything, but the look on his face told her everything she needed to know. "I did everything I could."

"I know," Cassie said, with tears in her eyes. Everything she'd been trying to prevent had happened. She'd killed her sister by coming back. She shook her head. "I did this."

"What?" Pycot answered, surprised. "You didn't do any of this. Ami did, and you had a chance to stop her, but not like this. Your sister would want you to finish it." He held the stone to her. "Get it to touch her."

Cassie wrapped her fingers around the stone. It carried a soft hum, like it was holding power, but not the power she was used to. This was dark and heavy. She pushed the feeling away and nodded.

She took a breath and kicked the door in. Ami was standing in front of the boy with Carik on his knees beside her.

"I had a feeling you would try something stupid," Ami said, pulling Carik closer to her. Ami's eyes slid to the stone in Cassie's hand.

"Let them go," Cassie demanded.

"Cody couldn't even kill me with that. You think you can?" Ami said, lowering her head to Carik's neck. She inhaled deeply and glanced back at Cassie. "I'll kill him before you even take a step."

Cassie glanced at Carik. He was calm and steady. Something Cassie wished she could be more of. "I'm sorry," she whispered.

She raced toward Ami. Every step seemed to take forever. Everything ran in slow motion. She watched as Ami lowered her head, her teeth grazing Carik's skin. Cassie was almost to her, but she wasn't fast enough. Ami's teeth dug into Carik's neck. Blood ran down his body.

Cassie grabbed Ami's arm and pulled herself into her, pulling her from Carik. As she slammed into Ami, she pushed the stone into her chest. When they hit the ground, Cassie rolled to the side and Ami pulled herself to her feet. She glanced down at her chest and watched the stone pull itself into her.

She snapped her gaze to Cassie. "What did you do?"

"I gave you what you wanted, to be free," Cassie said, crawling backwords on the floor.

Ami swallowed hard as the area around the stone started dissolving into dust. It radiated outward until her whole body turned to dust and fell to the ground. The stone dropped and bounced on the cement in front of the pile of dust.

Cassie stared at it for a moment before turning to Carik laying on the ground. Pycot had already turned him on his side and was holding pressure to his wound. She rushed towards him and looked at Pycot.

"We have to get him out of here. He needs help," Pycot said. "I can take Carik to someone, but you need to get the boy out of here and go to Lark."

Cassie froze as he shifted to water, taking Carik with him and disappeared.

37

Lark

She felt a warm glow on her skin and smiled. Everything felt warm and loving, like the world had no pain and suffering. When she opened her eyes, she could see the world around her. It had a golden haze and looked like a field of wildflowers.

Lark laughed and ran her hand over the nearest flower. She held it in her hand for a moment, taking it in. The flower had the most beautiful long petals. She let go of it and continued walking. In the distance, she could see someone she thought was familiar. She kept her eyes on the figure as it came into view. Lark felt her heart flutter as she finally realized who it was.

Her mother.

She felt herself run towards her. Her mother was standing there with her dark hair shining in the fields' glow. She had a smile on her face and held her arms out for Lark.

She ran into her mother's arms and held her tightly.

Lark felt her mother's arms wrap around her. Something she hadn't felt in so long. "I missed you so much."

"I know, baby," her mother said, still holding her. "I've been waiting for you."

Lark didn't want to, but pulled herself back. "Mom, where am I?"

Her mother smiled and cocked her head, something she'd done so many times when she was alive. "I guess it could be called heaven."

Lark shook her head as she registered where she was. "I'm dead?"

Her mom nodded, "but there is more to it than that."

"What do you mean, and what about Cassie?"

Her mother bit her lip. "There is a lot you don't know about who you are. Who you both are."

"Then tell me," Lark said.

Her mother grabbed her hand and held it. "We won't have time for that, but you need to know you are capable of everything you're about to face. Everything you think you can't do, you can. You and your sister were meant to be special."

Lark shook her head. "I don't want to be special."

"I know." Her mother said. "But you can't change your fate."

Lark tried to memorize her mother's face. The way the light hit her hair and the way her eyes seemed to always have a spark in them, but the light was fading. The darkness that she'd just emerged from was threatening to swallow them.

"What's happening?" Lark asked. She looked at the flowers as they withered around her.

"I love you," her mother said as the darkness overtook everything around her.

Lark opened her eyes and blinked. The darkness of the night sky was the only thing she could see with a dot or two of stars. She felt the cold ground beneath her and the air in her lungs.

She turned her head slightly, and Cassie was sitting there with her back to her. She could hear her crying and put her hand on her back. Cassie spun around, ready to kill whatever was touching her. Her eyes were filled with sadness, but once she registered what was happening, confusion ran across her face.

"What?" Cassie whispered.

"Cassie," Lark managed.

Cassie ran her hand over Lark's arm. "You're alive." She shook her head in confusion. "How?"

"I don't know." Lark said. She suddenly remembered the gapping hole in her body and ran her hand down her abdomen. There was nothing there, but some old dried blood. She sat up slowly and Cassie hurried to help her.

"Go slow," Cassie said as she put her hands around Lark. She pulled her into a hug and held her there. "I thought I'd lost you," she whispered.

"No, you will never lose me, Cassie." Lark leaned into the hug and closed her eyes. In that moment, it didn't matter how she'd come back or why, only that she was there with her sister and she wasn't going to squander that.

38

Cassie

Lark and Cassie made their way back to the Order of Fate and surveyed the damage. It was going to take a lot to fix this mess, but they had nothing but time. Ami was dead, and they had time to breathe.

"It won't last, you know," a familiar voice said from behind her.

Cassie smiled as she spun around. Carik was standing there, looking good as new. He even had that smile she'd decided wasn't such a bad thing on him.

"I'm so glad you're okay. I'm sorry," she said.

"For what? You did what you had to do." He raised an eyebrow. "And it all worked out."

Cassie bit her lip and Carik moved closer.

"What is it?" he said. "You look like there's something else."

She sighed. "There is. I finally know what's coming and we have to prepare for it." She glanced at Lark. "It's going to take all of us to save the future."

The dark warehouse was silent except for the dripping of water somewhere. It echoed in the old metal building. In the corner next to Ami's old bed was a crumpled body drained of blood, but its fingers curled against the cold cement.

The blue stone still sat in front of the pile of ash. It gave a faint glow, and the fingers inched towards it.

I can save you.

The hand latched onto the stone and pulled it to them.

Evil never dies.

To Be Continued...

ALSO BY TAVITA LANE

The Order of Fate Series

Blood and Magick

Magick Thief

Night Magick

Destiny of Magick

Moon River Mates Series

Blood Magick

Wolf Magick

Hunters Series

Burn

Hunt

Silver

Unforgiven

www.ingramcontent.com/pod-product-compliance
Lightning Source LLC
Chambersburg PA
CBHW052008150726
47999CB00004B/1578